Hometown Roots

LOST CANYON RANCH
BOOK ONE

CRYSTAL JOY

Hometown Roots

Lost Canyon Ranch
Book 1

Written by Crystal Joy

Edited by Janice Boekhoff at Lost Canyon Editing

Cover Design: Lyndsey Lewellen

www.crystaljoybooks.com

❀ Created with Vellum

Dedication

For Landon—always be open to a new path. It might be
the road you were meant to take all along.

CHAPTER

One

LAINEY EVANS INHALED the fresh Montana air while Jingle Bells trotted at a steady pace beneath her. There was no better way to start the day than taking a ride on her favorite horse. Eagles soared across the orange and yellow sky as the sun rose above the mountains. Water rushed by in Piney Creek, the gentle sound competing with the high-pitched melodies of robins and the rustle of wild animals awakening.

Lainey grinned and dug the heels of her well-worn boots into the palomino's sides. "Come on, Bells. Let's go faster."

Jingle Bells transitioned into a gallop, her strong muscular legs propelling them across the long stretch of land sandwiched between their homestead and the

Pryor Mountain Range. A brisk breeze blew across Lainey's cheeks.

If only she could take a longer ride. Head up into the woods and dip her toes in one of the icy cold ponds along the trails.

But duty called, even on a holiday. Thanksgiving dinner would be ready at four. Before then, she had a long list of chores to finish: stalls had to be mucked, the horses needed hay and water, eggs had to be collected from the chicken coop, five wooden boards on the round pen needed to be replaced, and preparations for the upcoming cattle drive had to be finalized with their ranch hands.

The to-do list would never get accomplished if she didn't start soon, and Grandpa was probably wondering why she wasn't back yet.

Sighing, she signaled for Jingle Bells to slow down and directed her mare toward the barn.

As they neared the large paint-chipped building, she dismounted from Bells and fed her horse a peppermint. "I promise we'll go on a trail ride real soon, girl."

Bells's ears perked with excitement.

Inside the barn, Grandpa's head popped up over Rebel's stall. "Morning, Lainey-girl." He bent over, scooped spoiled bedding from the floor onto a steel fork, and dropped it into a wheelbarrow. "Happy Thanksgiving."

"Same to you, Grandpa. How are you feeling today?"

He winked. "Like a newly oiled machine."

She chewed on the inside of her cheek. Was Grandpa telling the truth? Three months ago, he'd suffered from a heart attack. He'd recovered quickly, taking on the same workload within a couple of weeks after coming home from the hospital. *The ranch won't run itself*, he'd said. No one had argued with him—not Lainey or her youngest sister, Quinn, or their mom. Even with the addition of their ranch hands, there was too much to do to lose an able body.

Lainey attached a rope to Bells's halter, securing the horse in place. She untacked the mare by taking the riding equipment off, then grabbed a brush and hair detangler. She usually groomed her horses before rides, but sometimes, she liked to do it afterward. She sprayed the hair product into the mare's mane, using quick firm strokes to remove the tangles.

"I have something I want to talk to you about." Grandpa leaned the manure fork against the wall and straightened his wiry frame.

"What is it?"

A gleam sparked in his denim-blue eyes. "I think it's time to start the horse training business. After my stay in the hospital … Well, it's given me a new take on life. If we don't do it now, we'll look back one day and wonder what would've happened if we'd actually done it."

She bit her bottom lip and ran her fingers through a particularly tight knot in Bells's mane. They'd discussed starting a horse training business for too many years to count. Cherry Creek definitely had a need for it. The neighboring property had a large training facility, but they only worked with thoroughbred horses.

Which was why people often brought their horses to Grandpa. Growing up, Lainey had learned a lot from him. More so in the last four years, after she'd come back from college and officially worked at Lost Canyon Ranch.

Excitement bubbled in her chest. "Are you sure?"

"Absolutely." A boyish grin spread across his weathered face. "We could do it, you and me. I'm sure of it."

Lainey returned his smile.

Before she could give him an answer, tires crunched along the driveway. Her brows pinched together. They weren't expecting any visitors. Both ranch hands had arrived before she'd taken Jingle Bells for a ride, and it couldn't be Cheyenne.

Her sister had called yesterday, cancelling her trip to spend a long weekend at the ranch. No surprise there. Cheyenne hadn't come home in two years.

A flicker of guilt pricked at Lainey's conscience. She was the reason her sister hadn't come home.

A car door slammed shut, followed by the sound of footsteps.

Grandpa peeked out the window. His bushy eyebrows rose. "What in tarnation is Floyd doing here? I thought he was going to his nephew's house today." He shook his head and gave Lainey a look of resignation. "We can talk about the business later." He walked out of the barn, his steps slower than usual.

Or maybe she was imagining it.

She put Jingle Bells out to pasture and met Grandpa and Floyd Isaacson in the driveway.

Floyd waved a wrinkled hand, signaling for them to come near the back of the horse trailer attached to his white Ford pickup.

Lainey hurried over and stood beside Grandpa.

"Sorry to bother you, but I didn't know where else to go. The vet drove to Billings this morning. Won't be back until Sunday." As a lawyer at Big Horn Attorney and Law, Floyd normally spoke with careful precision, but this time, his words came out rushed and jumbled. "I was on my way to my nephew's house when I drove by the old Mason place. I thought it was deserted, but I saw a flash of movement inside the barn. As I drove closer, I heard a horse in distress. That's when I found this abandoned mare. I drove back to my place, hitched up the trailer, and came straight here."

Floyd led a skinny brown mare out of the trailer. Dirt clumps clung to her mane and tail. Despite her gaunt appearance, her belly beneath was round.

Grandpa crouched down and examined the horse's belly and udder. He let out a low whistle. "She's pregnant."

A lump formed in Lainey's throat. This horse had been abandoned at a time when she most needed nurturing and care. An unhealthy mama could lead to having premature labor, and a premature foal would be at risk for deformities, difficulty breathing, or issues with its kidneys and muscles. If the animal lived at all.

Floyd rocked back on his heels. "Can you help her?"

"Of course." Grandpa stood, his knees cracking from the movement. "Lainey and I will keep a close watch on her."

"Thank you." Floyd clasped a hand on Grandpa's shoulder.

"Anything for you, buddy," Grandpa said.

As Floyd drove away from Lost Canyon Ranch, Lainey took the horse's lead rope and looked at Grandpa. A wide grin spread across her face. "Let's go for it. I'm all in on the business."

He started to smile, but seconds later, his face

contorted in pain. Despite the frigid temperature, sweat trickled down his forehead. He clutched the left side of his chest and doubled over, falling to the ground.

The blood ran out of her face. *No, no, no.* She knelt down beside him and screamed for her youngest sister. "Quinn! Call 9-1-1!"

———

Knox Bennett rose from his desk to stretch. Outside, the rain intensified, beating on the roof of his two-bedroom condo. Across the open living space, big drops splattered against the large floor-to-ceiling windows, concealing his view of downtown Seattle.

The dreary day was most likely disappointing to families who'd entertained the idea of outdoor activities on Thanksgiving. But Knox had planned to work. And why not? His parents were traveling across the country. Most of his friends were newly married and spending the holiday with relatives.

Sure, he could've called Diana to see if she had plans, but then she'd get the wrong idea. She would wonder if he'd changed his mind about being in a committed relationship.

He hadn't. He worked long hours and traveled too often to have a serious girlfriend. It wouldn't be fair to either of them.

He strode into his spacious industrial-styled kitchen, made a large cup of expresso, and went back to his desk. A message popped up on Microsoft Teams from Vince Richfield: *Do you have a minute?*

Knox responded affirmatively.

Thirty seconds later, his boss had set up a meeting.

Knox clicked on *Join* and sat up straighter as Vince's wide frame filled the screen.

"You know, most people are watching football and eating turkey today," Vince said. Even in his own home, his boss's voice had a booming quality to it, drenched with the power and confidence of being vice president of Mt. Point Development.

Knox chuckled. "I'll watch football later. I wanted to look at the blueprints for Sally's Smoothie Shop. My architectural team finished them yesterday. I also received the contract for the bookstore in Port Townsend, so I figured I'd get a head start on ideas."

Vince pounded his pudgy fist against the armrest of his leather chair. "That's exactly the kind of initiative I'm looking for."

Knox pushed his shoulders back and lifted his chin. "Thank you, sir."

At the end of the year, Vince would retire. His boss had made it clear that he preferred an internal replacement.

"I'm impressed with the success of your projects

lately. Especially the renovations in Maple Valley, Iowa. The bed-and-breakfast was a charming addition. Just what that little river town needed." Vince leaned forward, his large forehead coming so close to the camera that the pores on his face became noticeable. "You're one of the people I have my eyes on."

His lips pressed together. *One* of the people? How many others was his boss considering?

He shifted uneasily in his chair. Mt. Point Development had grown rapidly in the last decade as more and more business owners realized the benefits of working with a build-to-suit company. As a result, Vince had hired several new realtors, architects, property managers, and construction crews to keep up with demand.

There were a lot of great people to fill the position —he was big enough to admit it—but he'd pursued more development opportunities in the Northwest and Midwest than anyone else on his team. Plus, he had a success rate of ninety-five percent. His achievements had to count for something.

"The progress of our current projects will be vitally important as I finalize my decision." Vince's gaze flickered away from the camera as he seemingly searched for a file on his computer. "Including this potential project in Cherry Creek, Montana."

Knox scrubbed a hand over his clean-shaven jaw, hiding the displeasure from his face. He'd lived in

Montana until he was thirteen. Unlike most kids, he couldn't wait to move out of the state. No more eight-month winters stuck indoors or long, winding drives from city to city or wide-open spaces filled with farm equipment and smelly animals. How anyone could enjoy living in Montana was beyond him.

"Here are a few images of the property."

Several pictures appeared on his screen—an aging barn, silo, and house surrounded by plush green grass and a mountainous terrain in the distance. The decrepit buildings stood out in stark contrast to the exquisite landscape. Exquisite, that is, for anyone who didn't actually live there.

"It's called Lost Canyon Ranch," Vince said, his gaze returning to the camera. "It's owned by Paul McKinley, a man in his early sixties."

"What does Mr. McKinley want us to do?"

Vince steepled his fingers beneath his double chin. "Actually, it wasn't McKinley who contacted us. The potential client would like to be referred to as G. S."

"Why?"

Vince shrugged. "I promised the client that we would sign a nondisclosure, and there was no reason to worry that McKinley would find out their identity. But they insisted on anonymity until we own the property and can start building a dude ranch resort."

"A *dude* ranch resort?"

"Yes. With five cabins and a barn for trail horses."

His leg bounced up and down. How intriguing. His team had never built a dude ranch. "Did G. S. tell you anything about the property?"

"Yes, and it sounds like a great location. The mountains in the picture are part of the Pryor Mountain Range, which were named after Nathaniel Pryor from the Lewis and Clark Expedition. You can see four other mountain ranges from the homestead—the Beartooths, the Big Horns, the Wind Rivers, and the Absarokas. There are also hiking trails that travel from the ranch up into the mountains." Vince licked his lips. "One of them leads to a spot where hikers or horseback riders can get a view of the first horse range established in the US. The wild horses can be seen grazing in a canyon on the eastern side of the mountains."

Knox raised his eyebrows. "It sounds like the perfect spot for a vacation getaway."

Vince nodded. "It has a lot of potential. I need you to contact the city and see if it's possible to rezone the property. It's currently a private cattle ranch. If it can be rezoned, I'd like you on-site as soon as you get confirmation."

"You got it." Knox saved the images to his desktop. He'd need to find out everything he could about Lost Canyon Ranch. Current acreage, number of livestock, debt-to-income ratio. If he could get enough data on his side, he'd be able to close the deal quickly and get the resort started. The faster he accomplished those tasks, the better his chances were of getting the promotion. "Is there anything obvious that would prevent Mr. McKinley from selling?"

Vince frowned, deepening the creases around his mouth. "It's doing well financially, and it has been in their family for three generations. Mr. McKinley has one daughter and three granddaughters, so it's possible he plans to bestow the land to any of them in the future."

"Oh." In other words, Mt. Point Development would have to make a compelling offer.

Vince turned his head and spoke to someone at home, then looked back at Knox. "I'm needed in the kitchen. Don't work too hard. I'll see you on Monday." The screen went black, signaling the end of the meeting.

Knox rose from his chair and pushed back his shoulders. Montana was the last place he wanted to go, but if he could obtain the property and get started on the resort, this could be *the* project to set him apart from his colleagues.

This opportunity was exactly what he'd been waiting for. If he received a promotion to vice president, his hours would be more manageable and he wouldn't have to travel as often. With a consistent schedule, he could pursue a serious relationship. He could finally get married and start a family.

A smile tugged at his lips. Everything he'd planned for the future was within reach. All he had to do was ensure that the Lost Canyon Ranch project was a success.

CHAPTER
Two

STILL WEARING her black dress and stock cowgirl boots, Lainey trudged inside the barn. She couldn't go into the house. Not yet. Now that Grandpa's funeral was over, neighbors would be stopping by with meals and casseroles all afternoon. Although many of them had good intentions, she wasn't in the mood to talk to them.

It still didn't seem possible that Grandpa was gone. Shortly after he'd arrived at the hospital, his heart had given out completely. Mom had quickly planned a celebration of life with help from friends in town, and Cheyenne had flown in from Nashville on a private jet.

Lainey scowled. At the funeral, people wouldn't stop staring at her sister. They should have been focusing on the service. It was the decent thing to do, a way to honor Grandpa and his life. Apparently, famous country singers took precedence.

People were overrated. Animals, on the other hand, made life better.

Clip-clop. Clip-clop.

Lainey peered inside the pregnant mare's stall. "Hi, Nutmeg." After she'd washed the dirt and grime off the horse earlier, her coat now looked like Lainey's favorite holiday spice. With Christmas about four weeks away, the name seemed fitting.

The mare looked up from her feed bucket, hay sticking out of her mouth as she chewed.

Nutmeg's appetite was a good sign. But would it be enough to keep her and her foal from having health issues? It was too soon to tell. Once the vet was back in Cherry Creek, she'd make an appointment for him to come out and check on the horse.

Across the barn, Rebel made a drawn-out, high-pitched whinny.

Her chest constricted. Rebel missed Grandpa. Unlike Nutmeg, the gelding had refused to eat. Moisture built in her eyes. She pulled the brim of her cowgirl hat lower over her forehead. Showing emotion was about the biggest sin you could commit as a female rancher.

Pushing her emotions away, she walked into the feed room at the back of the barn and grabbed an empty pail. She added dry wheat bran, chopped carrots, grain, and beet pulp, then topped off the mixture with water. She stirred and waited for it to thicken. Hopefully, Rebel would try a few bites.

She glanced down at the bran mash. The consistency compared to thick soup. Perfect. She carried it to Rebel's stall and unlatched the gate.

After not eating for two days, he had to be starving.

She put the pail up to his black-and-white-spotted muzzle. He sniffed the bucket, then turned his head away, uninterested.

Her heart sank. "You have to eat, boy. Grandpa would want you to." She set the bucket on the floor and placed a peppermint in the palm of her hand. He sniffed it but made no attempt to gobble up the treat.

Her shoulders slumped. She stuffed the candy in her coat pocket and gently massaged Rebel's ears, using light circular motions. He gave a soft nicker.

At least she could comfort him. That was something.

Footsteps approached the barn, followed by a husky voice. "Hello? Is anyone in here?"

Her hands stilled on Rebel's ears. So, the parade of funeral-goers had begun. Or maybe it had already started, and she hadn't been paying attention.

"I thought I heard someone talking," the man added quietly, as if he were talking to himself.

"Coming." She kissed Rebel, shut the stall, and

stepped out into the middle aisle.

A tall, broad-shouldered man stood in the open doorway, wearing a crisp dark suit, tie, and dress shoes. His chestnut hair was styled in an undercut with thick waves swept back. He had a clean-shaven face with a slightly large nose and piercing deep-set eyes that matched the color of his hair.

Her lips parted. Who was *he*? She'd never seen him before, and he hadn't been at Grandpa's funeral. But then, why was he dressed in a suit? There were only three reasons anyone in Cherry Creek ever wore formal clothing: church, weddings, or funerals. Had he come for Grandpa's funeral and missed it?

He stepped farther into the barn. His nose wrinkled, but he recovered quickly; his expression becoming stoic and unreadable. Beneath long dark lashes, his eyes sought hers. "Good afternoon. I'm Knox Bennett."

She shook his hand, his smooth, uncalloused skin very different from her own. He wasn't a rancher, not with that soft, baby-butt skin. Maybe he was one of Grandpa's business connections, like the grocer who bought their beef.

"You missed the funeral," she blurted.

His eyebrows pinched together. "Oh." It almost sounded like a question, but not quite.

"If you'd like me to get you a program, we have a few left. I can get you one."

"Uh, no. That's … all right." Knox shifted his weight from one foot to the other, seemingly at a loss for words.

She tugged on her dress. He looked confused. Maybe he didn't know. "Grandpa died. He had another heart attack."

Knox tilted his head to the side ever so slightly.

"Sorry. You probably knew my grandpa as Paul McKinley."

A few beats of silence passed before Knox spoke. "Mr. Kinley *died*?"

She nodded.

He opened his mouth, then closed it. "I'm sorry for your loss."

She'd heard this over and over again at the funeral, but for some reason, hearing it from this stranger brought grief to the surface. Two stray tears trickled down her cheeks. She turned to wipe them away. "Thank you." She choked out the words.

Suddenly, Rebel stuck his head out of the stall, his ears perked with curiosity. His neck extended so far that his muzzle was inches away from the stranger.

Knox froze, his arms stiff at his sides. "Oh, hello."

Rebel moved his muzzle closer to Knox, sniffing his suit jacket. Knox's cologne must have bothered the horse because the animal pulled back, shook his black mane, then sneezed.

Knox put a hand over the spot where Rebel had

sniffed and sneezed, then he slowly moved his hand away from his suit jacket. Slobber and stringy discharge clung to his palm, hanging in frothy ropes from his fingers. His lips formed a disgusted grimace. "Not on my nice suit," he mumbled.

Lainey laughed—the foreign sound shocking and relieving all at once. Her emotions were all over the place. But she couldn't help it. The repulsion on his face was funny. This guy had to be from the city. She grabbed a towel from a pile they kept on a bench and tossed it to him. "Here."

He dabbed the towel on his suit jacket, the scowl still plastered to his face.

"It's just drool. It won't stain."

"Right." He draped the towel over the stall door. "I'll come back another time." He turned and strode out of the barn as quickly as he'd come.

She stood still for a moment before questions started forming. "Wait!" she yelled. "Why are you coming back? What do you need?" Her questions were left unanswered, muffled by the sound of his car speeding out of the driveway. Dust from the gravel rose in gray puffy clouds.

She removed her hat and scratched her head, adding up the details. Expensive-looking suit and tie. Not familiar with horses. Unaware that Grandpa had passed away.

A sinking feeling settled in her gut. Whatever his

reason was for coming to Lost Canyon Ranch, it wasn't good.

———

Two loud knocks rapped on the motel door.

Knox threw off the thin sheets and stumbled out of bed. He rubbed his dry, tired eyes. It had been hard to sleep last night with images of the woman in the barn still etched in his mind—the dark circles beneath her bloodshot eyes, her red, tear-stained cheeks, the faded lipstick on her naturally pink lips.

Beneath her apparent anguish, she was undoubtedly beautiful. Blond wavy strands had escaped from her braid, framing her heart-shaped face. She had a strong chin and aquiline nose that suggested she was determined, but the soft curves of her mouth and delicately shaped eyebrows gave her a sweet, feminine appearance that had kicked him right in the gut.

It had been hard to look away from her and even harder to walk away. But it hadn't been the right time to ask about the property, not on the day of her grandpa's funeral.

He would have to go back. Hopefully, she'd be there. He should have asked for her name. Other questions surfaced as well—questions that didn't matter but somehow weighed on his mind. Did she live on the ranch? She'd seemed comfortable in the barn. Did she work for her grandpa? In either of those scenarios, she would lose part of her livelihood if Mt. Point Development bought the land.

Two loud knocks rapped on the door again.

"Just a second." Who would be knocking on his door this early? Sunlight peeked through the curtains, but it couldn't be later than seven, or his alarm would've gone off.

He grabbed his folded jeans from the desk chair and pulled them on quickly over his boxer briefs. As he opened the door, cold air rushed into the room. Shivers ran down his bare chest.

A burly man with a long, thick beard stood on the sidewalk, blocking the doorway. He thrust a paper at Knox.

"What's this?" Knox asked.

"Your bill."

He glanced down at the paper. "You must be mistaken. I'm not checking out today."

"Sorry, Mr. Bennett. The Lucky Motel's closing for good. The owner can't keep up with it. You have to leave."

"But this is the only motel in Cherry Creek."

"Can't stay open just for you. You're a business guy. You should understand." He turned and lumbered down the sidewalk toward the lobby.

Knox pinched the bridge of his nose. Paul McKinley—the man he'd come to Montana to talk to

—had died, and now the motel was closing. Not a great start.

He shut the door and undressed, heading toward the bathroom. He needed a hot shower and a new game plan. At this point, the biggest hurdle was connecting with the future owner of Lost Canyon Ranch.

Did Paul McKinley have a will? That would make transferring possession of the land happen much quicker.

In the meantime, he could find out who the next owner of the ranch *might* be. With only nine hundred residents, someone in Cherry Creek had to know. If there was one thing he'd learned about small towns, there was always a person who made a career out of knowing other people's business.

An hour later, Knox parked his rental—a Ford F-150—on Main Street in front of the Wagon Wheel Café. The morning might have gotten off to a bad start, but at least he was minutes away from a cup of coffee.

He stepped out of the truck. So, this was downtown Cherry Creek. Faded awnings hung above many of the shop's windows. Blue aluminum siding covered half of the storefronts, while the other buildings were built with dark wood or chipped bricks.

A woman wearing a Santa hat and a fluffy green sweater bent over a sign that advertised Christmas apparel. Across the street, a man set buffing towels and a bottle of shoe polish next to a chair. Within seconds, a man dressed in a thick puffy coat eased into the chair, propping his dress boots on the foot pedals.

Knox did a double take. A shoe-shining booth? Aluminum siding? Awnings? Downtown needed a complete facelift—new siding, roofs, windows, and doors. Hypothetically, this was a problem. With a dude ranch resort on the outskirts of town, visitors would want to shop here.

If it were up to him, his team would tear down the awnings. They'd put up vinyl siding in a variety of tan shades like Almond, Northern Oak, and Redwood, which would make the storefronts more aesthetically pleasing while keeping neutral tones that resembled the original buildings. Remodeling each business would make a big difference and add more appeal for travelers.

Would the mayor be open to discussing a remodel? Sam Sutherland had seemed nice enough on the phone when Knox called to ask about rezoning. The mayor sounded excited about a resort and said rezoning wouldn't be an issue. As long as Paul McKinley was open to selling. Knox's excitement had dissipated at that statement. Sam hadn't sounded too certain about the likelihood of the ranch changing ownership even while Mr. McKinley was alive.

But the mayor didn't know what Knox was capable of. He would do anything to get this deal to go through.

That is, after he had caffeine.

He stepped inside the Wagon Wheel Café. Holiday music played from speakers strung along the ceiling. Strings of colorful twinkling lights hung from the whitewashed wood walls and bordered the various paintings of wagons. Red buffalo plaid covered the seating areas of the booths. The scents of bacon, fried potatoes, and freshly brewed coffee hung in the air. His mouth watered as he stopped at the front counter.

A petite waitress with short curly hair wiped her hands on the stained apron wrapped around her tiny waist. Using her pointer finger, she pushed pink rhinestone-studded glasses higher up on her nose, assessing him like an unknown specimen. "I've never seen you before. What brings you to this neck of the woods? You aren't doing anything illegal, are ya?" Wrinkles creased the sides of her bright red lips as her mouth formed a thin line.

Whoa.

"I'm just messing with you." Her features softened, and a warm smile spread across her face, exposing lipstick on her two front teeth. "Hiya, Pumpkin. I'm Georgia. What can I get you to drink?"

"I'll have a latte with almond milk and expresso."

"Sugar Dumplin', I don't know where you think you are." Georgia turned and gestured to the chalkboard on the wall. A short list of options was written below *Coffee*. "We don't make lattes, and we certainly don't have almond milk."

He should have known. Five minutes in Cherry Creek had made one thing quite clear—this town was about as outdated as a rotary telephone. He sighed. "I'll have a coffee with creamer."

She handed him a menu. "Anything for breakfast?"

"Yes." After sitting down on a stool, he quickly read the double-sided paper that was stained with grease. "I'll have two eggs, sunny side up, and a side of hash browns."

"Be back in a jiffy."

"Thank you." While he waited, he turned around on the stool and rested his elbows on the counter. Several people glanced his way.

Oh, small towns. Some people welcomed him with open arms, intrigued and excited about whatever project he planned to execute. Many people remained leery, as if he was a villain preparing a vicious takeover. Only time would tell which category the people of Cherry Creek would fall in once they discovered why he was here.

Biting back a smile, he ignored their obvious

interest and looked at a flyer taped to the inside of the door.

Christmas Blade Parade. December 2-3. Beginning at 5 p.m.

Hmm. Good to know. Socializing with towns-people was a good idea before starting any project. If he could establish a relationship with the locals, they tended to be more supportive of his plans.

He lost sight of the flyer as a redheaded woman entered the café. She removed a long black coat, revealing tight jeans and a low-cut blouse. She waved at a few people before she sat down on the stool next to him.

Georgia returned with a mug and two packets of creamer.

"Thank you."

"My pleasure, Honey Pie."

The redhead rolled her eyes and looked at Knox. "She does it to everyone. She'll call you a million food related nicknames until the right one sticks."

Georgia put a hand on her bony hip. "I wasn't aware that my nicknames bothered you, Ginger Snap. I could always call you Scarlett, like everyone else, but what would be the fun in that?"

"You're right," Scarlett said. "No fun. And thanks

for asking—I'll have the egg burrito meal. Tell Owen not to burn the tortilla this time."

"You'll get what you get. If you have a preference, tell your fancy chefs at Serenity Stables to do a better job." Georgia marched into the kitchen, the double doors swinging behind her.

Knox stirred the powdered creamer in his coffee, smiling at their banter.

"Don't mind her," Scarlett said. "Georgia's a rose bush. Some days you see the roses, some days you get pricked by the thorns."

He took a sip of dark roasted coffee. "I'll keep that in mind."

She extended her hand. "Scarlett Sutherland."

"Sutherland. Are you related to Sam, the mayor?"

She nodded. "That's my dad."

Perfect. Anyone related to the mayor would be a good person to have on his side.

Scarlett turned toward Knox and crossed her legs. "So, what brings a clean-cut man like you to Cherry Creek?"

"I'm here on business."

"Will you be staying awhile?" she asked.

"Possibly. It depends on how long my project takes."

She made an obvious glance down at his ringless left hand. "That must be hard on your girlfriend. Not knowing when you'll be back, I mean."

Heat flushed beneath his cheeks. The redhead was quite friendly. "Can I ask you a question?"

"Of course."

"What might happen to Lost Canyon Ranch now that Mr. McKinley has passed away?"

Scarlett shifted on the stool and uncrossed her legs. "I'm guessing the land will be handed down to his daughter, Josephine."

Georgia bustled out of the kitchen, set down their plates, and refilled his coffee.

"If I were Josephine, I'd sell it," Scarlett continued, peering down at her long, rounded fingernails. "Josephine lives on that huge property with two of her daughters. The three of them can't possibly run the ranch alone. Even with a couple of ranch hands, it's too much to handle."

"I see."

A hunchbacked man with a cane rose from a nearby table and tossed the newspaper on the counter. "See you tomorrow, Georgia."

Knox glanced down at the paper—the *Crack of Dawn News*. One of the front page articles read "Fist Fights at the Outlaw Saloon at an All-Time High. Cherry Creek's Sheriff Blames Drug Use."

Georgia followed his gaze. "Downright shame. First, the Lucky Motel, now the Outlaw Saloon. Soon enough, the bar will have to close down too."

"What do you mean?" Knox asked, scooping eggs onto his fork.

Georgia took off her glasses. She lifted her apron and cleaned the lenses. "The motel had to close because the sheriff's department kept arresting people there for drug trafficking. No one wanted to stay there anymore."

Scarlett scoffed. "No. That's not true. That place was going downhill way before any illegal activity took place, and you know it."

He mixed his eggs into his hash browns and took another bite as Georgia and Scarlett argued about the downfall of the Lucky Motel. If criminal activity had negatively impacted the motel, it could also affect the dude ranch resort.

And yet, by the time the resort was up and running, Mt. Point Development would no longer own it. Their client would take ownership as soon as it was completed and the city agreed they were up to code.

And if that happened, it meant the woman he'd met yesterday would lose her home. She must be one of the granddaughters living at the ranch with her sister and mom.

An unsettling feeling wormed its way into his gut. He'd be the one taking it away from her.

But he couldn't worry about her feelings. He had a job to do.

CHAPTER
Three

ON MONDAY, Lainey made true to her promise and rode Jingle Bells on a wide trail up the Pryor Mountains. After her great-grandfather had inherited the land, he'd created several paths through the woods. Many would consider it rough terrain, but the horses were used to it. Large junipers, Douglas firs, limber pines, and a few groves of aspens surrounded them on both sides.

Up ahead, the trail split in two directions. Lainey pulled on the reins, choosing left, which went closer to Piney Creek. She rolled her shoulders and took deep breaths in and out, waiting for the tension in her shoulders to lessen. But even a ride through the mountains couldn't shake the stress pressed tightly into her muscles.

What would Grandpa's will say?

Before she could contemplate it for too long, her cell phone rang with "Blue Christmas." The song lasted for three seconds, then the call dropped. She glanced down at the screen. *Missed call from Cheyenne.*

A minute later, a text came through.

Where are you? We have a meeting with the lawyer at 9.

As if Lainey needed a reminder.

No doubt Cheyenne was ready to get the meeting over with. It was the only reason her sister hadn't left yet. Once the will was read, Cheyenne would hightail it out of here and head back to Nashville to start her next record.

Her sister didn't care about the ranch. Cheyenne had made that quite clear when she'd moved out at eighteen without a backward glance.

Waves of uncertainty rolled through her stomach. Grandpa had most likely entrusted the land to her mom. But what if Mom didn't want the responsibility of owning Lost Canyon Ranch?

When Dad took off fifteen years ago, Mom had stepped up and done everything she could to raise Lainey and her younger sisters and also help out around the ranch. She never complained, but her passion for ranching had left along with Dad.

Lainey couldn't let her mom give it up. Especially

since Grandpa had wanted to open the horse training business here.

She hadn't told her family about her last conversation with him. It hadn't seemed important with more pressing issues to discuss, like planning his funeral, but now, it weighed heavily on her mind. Would her family be supportive of the new business, or would they have doubts? Without Grandpa, they might not see the point. *He* was the horse whisperer.

Before her own doubts could sweep in, she slipped her phone into her pocket and redirected Bells toward the barn. "Time to go home, girl."

Twenty minutes later, Lainey put Bells out to pasture and started toward the house.

Cheyenne rose from the porch swing and crossed her arms. "Finally." As she walked, her nude high heels clicked against the paint-chipped porch, and her long blonde curls bounced across a navy lace dress with a ruffled hem. "What were you thinking, going out for a joyride this morning? You knew we had this meeting."

Lainey ran her tongue along her teeth. "Bells needed to get out. I wasn't planning on being gone too long."

"You could've done it later."

"I don't know why you're upset. It looks like you found a productive way to spend the morning." She gestured with her hands. "Why are you so dressed up? Your fancy clothes could easily get ruined. Or have you been gone so long you've forgotten what it's like to live on a ranch?"

Cheyenne narrowed her eyes. "You know exactly why I haven't been home. Or have you forgotten what you said to me last time I visited?"

"I didn't say it to *you*. I said it to your hoity-toity boyfriend. And I'm glad I told Damian never to come back. It obviously worked. He's not here."

Cheyenne bit down on her bottom lip, removing some of the glossy red hue covering her full lips.

Quinn honked the horn of her rusted black pickup. She stuck her head out the open window, her long brown hair swept beneath a worn baseball cap. "Would you two cut it out? Cheyenne, you *are* way too dressed up, and Lainey, I'm sure you smell like a horse. But we don't have time for either of you to change or clean up, so let's get going." She sank back into the driver's seat, then yelled, "And neither one of you better argue with me about driving!" She glanced at Mom, sitting in the passenger's seat. "Mom said I could. I'll get us there the fastest."

Lainey rolled her eyes. *As long as we get there in one piece.* Quinn's driving skills were questionable—resulting in two crooked stop signs. But there was no use arguing about it now.

Thirty minutes later, they walked inside Big Horn

Attorney and Law. Floyd met them at the front doors, giving each of them a hug.

"Come on in." He gestured toward his office.

The lingering smell of stale coffee filled the small space. Heads of a big horn sheep, a wolf, and a moose protruded from the back wall—trophies from the days Floyd and Grandpa had hunted together.

Floyd shut the door. He eased down into his chair, his brown eyes misting. "I know I already said this at the funeral, but I'm sorry for your loss. Paul was a good man. As someone who'd been friends with him for all of my adult life, I can tell you with certainty that he loved you very much."

Cheyenne shifted in her chair, and Quinn sniffled.

Lainey removed her hat and placed it over her heart—her way of acknowledging Floyd's kind words.

"Before we get started with the logistics, I have to know. How is the mare doing?" he asked.

"I named her Nutmeg. She's doing a little better and eating a lot, which is great. But I'm concerned it's too late and her low weight will cause her to go into labor."

"Will you keep me posted?"

"Of course."

Floyd blew his nose. "Thank you."

He leaned to the side and tugged open a drawer with shaky hands. "I have something to show all of you." He took out a piece of paper and four envelopes, setting them on his desk.

She glanced down at the paper. Grandpa's handwriting filled the page. What was that? Certainly, not an official will.

"Paul's first heart attack was a wake-up call. After all these years of me telling him to write a will and take care of his affairs, he finally listened to me. In addition to his will, he wrote a letter expressing his last wish for your family."

Floyd straightened to his full height, his long frame well above the back of his chair. First, he looked at Mom, then he picked up Grandpa's letter and began reading. "To my beautiful daughter, Josephine: You've always put others before yourself. Leave all responsibilities at the ranch and take a trip. Visit somewhere you've always wanted to go."

Floyd handed Mom an envelope. "Paul had a separate fund saved for you to do this. It's not much, but it's enough for you to travel for several weeks."

Mom clasped a hand over her mouth. "You can't be serious. I mean, I couldn't do that. I can't leave my girls right now."

"Yes, you can," Lainey said. "Grandpa wanted you to. You deserve this."

Mom noticeably swallowed and nodded.

Floyd turned to Quinn, held up the next envelope, and continued reading from the letter. "To my racing queen: Take this money and pay for that show jumping coach you've always wanted to have. And don't forget, go big or go home."

Quinn reached for the envelope. A slow grin spread across her face. "Wow. That was really thoughtful."

Floyd eyed Cheyenne before he lowered his gaze to the letter and read. "To my nightingale: Bring your talent back to Cherry Creek. I realize you have plenty of your own money, but use what I've given you to do something special in this town."

Cheyenne didn't speak. She took the envelope, her face a mixture of confusion and sadness.

Floyd glanced at Lainey. "To my horse whisperer: Use this money to go toward our horse training business. I'll be with you every step of the way."

All eyes swiveled to Lainey.

Her chest rose and fell. He'd mentioned their business. Their dream. She opened her mouth to explain when Floyd continued.

"There's more. The last part of his wish is that Lainey, Cheyenne, and Quinn live at the ranch together for one month from the reading of this letter." He pointed a long bony finger at his desk calendar. "Which would be right after Christmas."

Floyd rested his forearms on his desk and clasped his hands together. "Paul wants you to work together and rediscover what made you a family. Once the conditional time has lapsed, you'll report back to me with your honest opinion of how it went. And of course, I'll be in the know. Nothing stays secret in Cherry Creek for long. Then, and only then, will you take ownership of Lost Canyon Ranch, and I'll read his will."

The cow-themed clock ticked loudly as silence filled the office.

Lainey's heart picked up speed. The ranch could be *hers*? Before excitement could set in, another thought emerged. What if they didn't meet Grandpa's standards? Who would get the land, then?

"Wait a minute …" Cheyenne gripped both sides of the chair tightly. "Why would he ask me to take a break from my career?"

Lainey expelled a frustrated breath. Bitter resentment rose like a nasty weed rooted deeply in place. "Are you serious? Grandpa gave us the opportunity to own the ranch and that's your response?"

Cheyenne rose, her face stark white. "I need some fresh air." She left the room, leaving them in silence once again.

Lainey slumped back in her chair. Even she had to admit, Grandpa's request *was* a lot to take in. It wasn't plausible for her and her sisters to work together or rediscover what made them a family in such a short amount of time.

In fact, they were more likely to fall apart.

———

Knox wound a thick scarf around his neck as he trekked up a hill on the outskirts of Lost Canyon Ranch. He had to get closer to the property. He'd been in town almost a week, eating at the Wagon Wheel Café and browsing through Buffalo Run Hardware or Cherry's Five and Dime. Unfortunately, no new information had surfaced since his first few days in town.

The least he could do was get a good look at the property and survey it himself. Professional assessors would still need to examine the land thoroughly, but with a good vantage point, he'd notice any glaring issues.

With one final stride, he stepped onto the top of the hill. Down below, a winding gravel driveway led to a large two-story log cabin. The exterior was faded from the sun, giving the cabin a dull, washed-out complexion. A decrepit red barn towered above the cabin, its shadow looming over a circular fenced-in pen. If the fence had once been level, it was hard to tell now—many pieces hung unevenly.

He scratched the back of his head. So much for being observant. He'd been so caught off guard by the beautiful woman in the barn and the news of Mr. McKinley's death that he hadn't noticed how bad off the ranch was.

But bad was good in this case. It made it more likely that the new owner would accept an offer from Mt. Point Development.

Excitement tingled in his chest. Despite the poor state of the buildings, it was easy to see why their potential client had chosen this location. The log cabin would be a perfect spot for the main office. The downstairs area could be an open floor plan with a cozy lobby and kitchenette, and the bedrooms upstairs could be the sleeping quarters for the manager of the resort.

Outside, there was easily enough space for four or five family-sized cabins to be built nearby. The barn would be torn down, replaced with a larger one that would fit at least a dozen trail horses.

Using his work tablet, he took pictures from different angles. This afternoon, he'd drive back to his new hotel in Red Lodge and draw a few design options. An architect would make the actual blue-prints, but his team sometimes shared tasks to get more accomplished at a quicker pace.

At the bottom of the hill, an engine turned off. He walked back to the other side of the hill and peered down. A black pickup truck was parked on the side of the road behind his vehicle. An older woman leaned against the passenger's side of the truck, talking on her cell phone, while three younger women marched up the hill in his direction.

One of them was the woman from the barn. She wore ripped jeans, an open leather jacket with a green plaid shirt beneath, and a brown cowgirl hat. Her blond hair was pulled back into a low ponytail.

His stomach did an unexpected flip-flop.

She didn't look too happy to see him. She wore a deeply etched frown, and her eyes narrowed. The brunette next to her wore a similar expression.

Yikes.

The third woman hadn't glanced at him yet. She stared at the ground as she carefully stepped through the ankle-high grass in high heels.

When she hit flatter ground, she finally lifted her gaze.

He blinked, then blinked again. Where had he seen her before?

The cowgirl stopped in front of him and folded her arms across her chest. "You again."

Tucking the tablet between his arm and side, he rocked back on his heels. "Howdy."

"What are you doing here?" she asked.

"It's a long story. Right now, I'm enjoying the view."

"Why?" Instead of letting him answer, she threw her hands in the air in an exasperated manner. "I mean, you're obviously not from Cherry Creek. You sped down our driveway. Do you know how dangerous that was? You could've hit one of our animals."

Heat rushed up the back of his neck. "I'm sorry. I didn't think about that."

The familiar-looking blond waved a manicured hand in front of her face. "You didn't answer my sister's question. Why did you come to Lost Canyon Ranch?" Curiosity, rather than skepticism, laced her tone.

That face. That voice. His eyes widened in recognition. "Are you Cheyenne Evans? *The* Cheyenne Evans?" Hopefully, he didn't sound like a crazed fan.

"Why, yes, I am." She gave a soft, delighted chuckle. "And these are my sisters, Lainey and Quinn." She pointed to each woman as she spoke.

Lainey. What a pretty name.

"We have a lot to do today, so I only want to ask this one more time." Lainey tapped a boot on the ground. "Why are you looking at our ranch?"

A bead of sweat trickled down his forehead. Wait a second. Had she said *our* ranch? "It's yours?"

Lainey exchanged a look with her sisters. "It will be soon, yes."

"Oh." His voice went up an octave as he tried to keep his composure. The ranch was going to the granddaughters instead of Mr. McKinley's daughter. This wasn't good. Lainey didn't like him, and now there were three women to convince instead of one.

Quinn put her hands on her hips. She stood a full foot shorter than her sisters, but when she spoke, her tone was assertive, making her seem taller than she was. "We deserve an answer, Mr. …"

"Bennett. Knox Bennett." His heart hammered hard and fast. The timing was all wrong. They'd just been informed they owned the land, and they were still grieving the loss of their grandpa.

But he had to tell them the truth, or they'd never trust him.

"I work for Mt. Point Development. My company would like to make a generous offer to buy your ranch. I can go over the exact numbers with you later today, but I'll tell you this up front—we're offering a lot more than what the ranch is worth." The words spilled out of his mouth like an inexperienced developer. What was wrong with him?

Lainey shook her head. She took a step closer, the scent of soap and leather drifting toward him. "Money doesn't define how much our land is worth. It's not for sale."

Cheyenne put her hand on Lainey's shoulder. "Maybe we should hear him out. It wouldn't hurt."

A flicker of hope surfaced. At least one of them was interested.

"No." Lainey's response left no room for question.

His jaw tightened. The conversation had gone all wrong.

He'd have to try again. He needed to convince one of them, who would then persuade the other two. But who would he start with?

Quinn looked like the youngest, so she might not hold as much weight when it came to family decisions. Maybe he could talk to Cheyenne since she was open to his offer. Or should he try to reason with Lainey since she was firmly against selling?

No matter who he chose, he wouldn't leave town until the land was signed over to Mt. Point Development.

CHAPTER

Four

THE SCREEN DOOR creaked as Lainey rushed out of the house. She quickly strode across the weathered porch, their border collie, Maximus, at her heels. With each step, the wooden floorboards groaned in protest. She really needed to grease the door and fix the floorboards, but those tasks would have to wait. Tori Sutherland's riding lesson was supposed to start five minutes ago.

She chewed on her already-bitten-down nails. This was gonna be awkward. Will Sutherland would probably drop off Tori. He was her dad, after all. But Lainey hadn't spoken to him in eight years. Not since they'd broken up before they left for college.

And now he was back. He'd moved to Cherry Creek three weeks ago after having gone through a nasty divorce. At least, that was what Georgia had said. Luckily, Lainey hadn't run into him. She'd seen his SUV driving by on his way to his parents' place, but that was it.

Then he'd texted her, asking if she'd give riding lessons to his daughter.

He must have felt awkward about this too since he'd texted instead of calling. So why had he chosen her as a riding teacher? She'd have to ask him.

Up ahead, a flash of red hair moved inside the round pen. *Uh-oh.* Was that Tori? Lainey quickened her pace, climbed over the fence, and jumped inside the round pen with Maximus following beside her, wagging his tail.

At first, Tori didn't notice Lainey. Instead, the five-year-old girl skipped toward Jingle Bells, who was bent over the trough, taking a drink.

"Tori, slow down," Lainey called. "You need to approach horses in a gentle manner so you don't scare them." She took a quick glance behind her. Where the heck was Will? He should know better than to leave his daughter alone with a horse.

She caught sight of a vehicle in her peripheral vision but then turned her full attention back when Bells whinnied. Tori's sudden movements had caused the mare to shoot backward, her ears standing high, nervous and alert.

Tori moved out of the mare's way. Her eyes were filled with delight rather than concern. She extended her arm and held out an apple. "Here, horsey horsey. I brought you a present."

The mare caught sight of the bright green fruit, trotted toward Tori, and gobbled up the treat within seconds.

Lainey frowned but kept her tone light. "You should've checked with me before you gave my horse something to eat."

"My aunt, Scarlett, told me that horses love apples. She said it would make the horse like me."

Lainey gritted her teeth. "That's true, but make sure you ask next time."

"Is there a problem?" Evelyn Sutherland stepped out of her Cadillac Escalade wearing a rose-colored blouse, a floral-print pencil skirt, and ostrich boots.

Ugh. Will had sent his mom to do the drop-off.

Maximus took one look at the mayor's wife and ran off toward the house with his bushy tail lowered to the ground. Even the dog didn't want to be around her. Not that she took any notice.

Evelyn sauntered over to the round pen and took off her Gucci sunglasses. "Did my granddaughter do something wrong?"

Lainey chewed on the inside of her cheek, debating what to say. Talking to the mayor's wife was worse than seeing her ex-boyfriend. Despite being neighboring ranchers, Sam and Evelyn had never gotten along with Lainey's family. After Lainey broke up with Will, Evelyn's dislike had intensified. According to rumors, Evelyn had told everyone in town that Lainey broke Will's heart.

Lainey cleared her throat. "You shouldn't let Tori go inside the pen until I'm with her. Even though Bells is a good horse, it's still dangerous."

Evelyn fingered the pearl necklace resting near her collarbone. "I don't see the issue. Tori has been riding the horses at our stables. She's a natural with animals, if I do say so myself." She stopped toying with the necklace and muttered loudly, "Why Will wanted *you* to give Tori lessons is beyond me. We have plenty of well-qualified trainers at Serenity Stables."

"I'd like to ask him that myself."

Evelyn opened her mouth, then shut it. "I'll be back to pick up Tori in an hour."

Good riddance. Lainey gave the mayor's wife a thumbs-up and turned to the girl. "Ready?"

"Yes." A wide grin spread across Tori's freckled face, showcasing a missing front tooth. She tugged on her tailored jacket and smoothed out her white breeches. "Will you let me wide weally fast? Can I do tricks? Is your sister weally Cheyenne Evans?"

"Yes, Cheyenne is my sister."

"Can I get her autogwaph?"

"I'll have to ask her."

"Oh." Tori's shoulders lowered. "OK."

Lainey smiled. "Today we'll stick with the basics. I'll teach you how to sit on the saddle, hold the reins, and give a few verbal signals."

"Did you date my dad? That's what he told me."

Lainey nodded. At this rate, they'll never get started on the lesson. She signaled for Bells to draw near and reached for the lead rope to hold the palomino still. "First, you always mount a horse from the horse's left. Stand on this mounting block, and slowly move your right leg up and over the horse's back."

Tori did as she was told and situated herself in the saddle, sitting up straight.

"Good. Let me adjust the stirrups."

Jingle Bells shifted uneasily; her ears pulled back.

"Steady girl," Lainey said.

"Why's she doing that? Doesn't she like me?" Tori asked.

"It'll be all right. Bells is just getting used to you." Lainey kept her voice calm and reassuring, not only for Tori's sake but for Bells's. The horse was abnormally skittish all of a sudden.

After settling the horse, Lainey showed Tori how to hold the reins. "When you want to go left, pull to the left. When you want to go right ..." She let the sentence trail off as Jingle Bells stomped her front hooves on the sandy surface. The horse shook her mane and flared her nostrils.

Lainey's eyebrows pinched together. She gripped the lead rope tighter.

Tori looked down at Lainey with alarm. "I want to get off. This horsey is scary."

"OK. Let me help yo—"

Jingle Bells took off with such force that the rope slipped through Lainey's fingers. The horse cantered to the opposite side of the pen, then circled around the perimeter of the fence.

Lainey's eyes widened. What was going on with Bells?

"Help!" Tori's voice was muffled against the horse as she clung to the animal's wide back.

"Whoa." Lainey jogged at a brisk pace, trying to catch up to them. If she could reach the lead rope or halter, she could stop Bells and get Tori off. But the horse was moving too fast. Lainey broke into a run, her arm outstretched, inches away from the rope.

The mare changed direction and took off in a straight line toward the fence.

"No, Bells. Don't!" Lainey yelled.

The horse lifted her front legs and jumped over the fence.

Tori's arms flailed in the air as she flew off the horse. The girl landed with a thud on her right side, her head barely missing the fence.

Lainey raced toward Tori and knelt beside the girl. "Are you OK?"

Trembling, the girl shifted to her back. She held her right arm at an odd angle. Her eyes watered with tears. "It huwts."

A car horn blared, followed by tires screeching across pavement. Seconds later, Evelyn's shrill scream pierced the air, muted by the sound of metal crashing.

"I'll be right back." Lainey sped down the driveway and turned onto the main road, assessing the accident.

Jingle Bells had jumped back over the fence, probably scared by the vehicle. The horse galloped across the fields, weaving between cattle, seemingly unharmed.

Good. At least Bells wasn't physically hurt. But what about Evelyn?

Steam rose from the front of her Cadillac, which had nose-dived into the shallow ditch. The driver's window was open, revealing a side view of Will's mom. Blood trickled down the woman's forehead.

A lump formed in Lainey's throat as she rushed to the vehicle. "Are you all right?"

Evelyn slowly moved her head in Lainey's direction. "No, I'm not. What kind of question is that? Your horse jumped in front of my car. I tried to stop so I wouldn't hit it but ended up swerving and going into the ditch. I should've hit the crazy animal instead."

Lainey winced. Thankfully, Evelyn hadn't thought of that earlier.

"Where's Tori?"

"I think her arm is broken. She fell off Jingle Bells right as the horse took off."

Evelyn pursed her lips. "People say you have your grandpa's gift, but your horse doesn't even listen to you."

She tried to swallow the lump in her throat, but it wouldn't budge.

Evelyn made a *humph* noise. "You'll be hearing from our lawyers."

Lainey squeezed her eyes shut for a moment. How was she supposed to start a horse training business when the mayor's wife would tell everyone in town about the accident?

But she couldn't think about that now. There were more pressing matters at the moment. "I'll call an ambulance."

As soon as it was on its way, she'd call the vet. Something was wrong with Jingle Bells.

———

Knox turned onto the highway, heading toward Cherry Creek. The one-hour commute from Red Lodge was doable for now. But if a snowstorm hit, it could be days before he'd be able to travel to Lost Canyon Ranch. Many rural roads were often left to the responsibility of landowners who had their own plows. Which was an obstacle his team would need to address when they built the resort.

If the resort got built at all.

How would he persuade the Evans sisters to sell? The more he thought about it, he had to rule out Cheyenne. She would be the easiest to convince, but based on her body language, Cheyenne didn't have a close relationship with her sisters. Which meant the charismatic country music star couldn't persuade them to change their minds.

That left only one choice. He'd have to get through to Lainey. Today, he'd see what he could find out about her. He'd start at the Wagon Wheel Café, then make his way to other places like the Bear Country Bakeshop, Cherry Creek Liquor store, and Big Pine Beauty Salon. He didn't need a haircut, but he'd get one anyway.

He rolled his shoulders and turned on the radio, trying to release the mounting tension in his muscles. Country station, country station, static, and … country station. Not current country music, like Cheyenne Evans's songs, but the old, twangy kind of country. "Take Me Home, Country Roads" played softly over the sound system.

These were country roads, all right. Not a house

or building in sight. Montana was exactly as he remembered it from childhood. Bleak and barren.

He turned off the radio. Probably for the best. He needed to call Vince and give his boss an update. He'd tried calling a few times, and not one call had gone through.

Even on the highway, his phone still only had two bars.

Someone needed to put in a cell tower nearby. How did people live with such spotty service? Hopefully, he'd be able to stay in touch with his team to check in on his other projects, like the smoothie shop in Seattle and the bookstore in Port Townsend.

He scrolled through his contacts and clicked on Boss Man.

Vince picked up on the second ring. "Hey, Knox. How's … going?"

"I've had some hiccups, sir. Mr. McKinley passed away, and the land is being given to his three grown granddaughters."

"The line's breaking up … Can't … Have … made the offer yet?"

Knox threw his hands up in irritation. Couldn't he have clear cell service for five minutes? "I haven't made an offer yet." He paused in case Vince had a response, but when none came, he continued. "I'm in uncharted territory. I've never dealt with property owners who've just inherited the land we want to buy. They're still mourning the loss of their grandpa."

"It's unfortun … timing, but don't take too long."

"Yes, sir. I understand."

"We want this deal to …" Vince's voice trailed off into silence.

Knox let out a low growl. He'd lost the call. What was Vince about to say? That he wanted the deal to go through? To exceed the company's annual quota? To add a dude ranch resort to their growing list of unique projects? Whatever he'd said, it was meant to put pressure on Knox to acquire the property.

Vince didn't need to put pressure on him. Knox put enough on himself.

Especially after watching most of his friends get married in the last two years. They were happy. Content. Moving on and ready to start families, while he was still a bachelor.

And Lainey Evans was standing in the way of his dreams coming to fruition. She didn't know it yet, but she and her sisters would sell him the ranch. He would make sure of it.

CHAPTER

Five

LAINEY LEANED against the doorframe of
Grandpa's bedroom. As the sun rose above the hori-
zon, its bright rays shone through the window, illu-
minating flecks of dust floating through the air. She
hadn't been in here in a week, not since the day of his
heart attack.

Pictures of Mom, Grandma, Lainey, and her
sisters sat on a nightstand next to his reading glasses,
weather radio, and thirty-year-old Timex watch. The
quilt Grandma had made him for their twenty-fifth
anniversary lay neatly over his comforter. Before
Mom left for her trip to Florida, she must've made
his bed. Grandpa certainly hadn't, he'd stopped
making his bed soon after Grandma passed away ten
years ago.

Lainey slowly walked into his room and pushed

the closet door to one side. His favorite overalls were right in the middle, next to his blue long-sleeve T-shirt. She pulled his shirt off the hanger and held it near her nose. Scents of dirt, cedar, and pipe tobacco still lingered on the fabric.

She closed her eyes and spoke quietly. "Grandpa, I miss you so much."

She fisted his shirt, a mix of anger and sadness woven so tightly together she couldn't decipher which emotion she felt more. The timing of his passing wasn't fair. It wasn't supposed to be this way. Sixty-three was far too young. He had so much more to do in this life, and it had all been ripped away from him. "How can I start our business on my own? It won't be the same without you. I don't know what I'm doing." She choked back a sob. "The only thing I know for sure is that I'm not giving up the ranch."

Especially not to some hotshot developer. An image of his pretty-boy face surfaced behind her closed lids. How could anyone be so unsympathetic? Grandpa's funeral had only been a week ago, and Knox Bennett was already swooping in and offering them money. What an inconsiderate jerk.

If that wasn't bad enough, Cheyenne's willingness to listen to the offer was even worse. How could her sister do that to her? To Quinn? This was their home.

She opened her eyes, put the shirt back on the

hanger, and closed the closet. No way would she let Knox take away the ranch. It was theirs to keep. A surprising gift to treasure. He might as well pack up and go home.

Vibrations buzzed inside her pocket, followed by the instrumental version of "Silent Night." She pulled out her cell phone. "Hello?"

"Hi, Lainey. It's Will."

Will? Why was her ex calling? Did he want to chew her out for Tori's and Evelyn's accidents? "I'm really sorry about your daughter's arm and your mom's car, I—"

"I know it wasn't your fault."

Huh?

Will cleared his throat. "I'm not sure what my parents have said to anyone in town or how much you've heard about me in the last several years, but I recently became a vet."

"Oh. I hadn't heard that." People usually avoided the topic of Will with her, and she never asked. Mostly to avoid the guilt.

When they'd broken up, he'd been on the verge of tears. She'd forced herself to look sad too. But as soon as he left, she'd taken her first easy breath in months. Their relationship had been all wrong from the start.

With their ranches eight miles apart, she'd grown up with him, his three brothers, and his sister, Scarlett. She'd always viewed him as a friend. When he asked her out, she didn't have the heart to say no. After that, she let their relationship go on for a year, hoping her feelings would change.

But it only made things worse. The pressure of staying together was too much, and finally, she'd ended it before they left for college.

"This might come as a surprise to you, but I'm taking over Dr. Zeke's practice. He received a job at a veterinary clinic in Billings. That's why I moved back to Cherry Creek."

Lainey lifted her eyebrows. "Wow. Congratulations."

"Thanks. Anyway, I called you because I have the test results for Jingle Bells."

She sat down on the edge of Grandpa's bed, her back rigid. *Please don't let anything be wrong with my horse.*

"Jingle Bells had cocaine in her system."

"Cocaine." Her pulse pounded in her ears. "As in, the drug?"

"Yes."

She leaned forward, resting her elbows on her knees.

"Dr. Zeke filled me in, and unfortunately, he's seeing a rising issue with cocaine in horses in this area. It happens most often when groomers do a line, don't wash their hands, then return to their daily tasks, like refilling a horse's water container or preparing food. The cocaine transfers from the person's hands to the horse's mouth by accident."

"Let me get this straight. Someone who did cocaine came into contact with Bells and accidently gave her some too?"

"That would be my guess, yes." Will blew an airy breath into the receiver. "However, it's also possible it was done on purpose. There have been cases when jockeys or owners inject cocaine into their racehorses to improve performance." He paused for a moment. "You don't use her for competitions, do you?"

"No, she's mainly a trail horse."

"We can probably rule that out, then. Do you remember everyone who came into contact with your horse that day?"

She pinched the bridge of her nose. "Quinn took care of the horses that morning before she left to meet her new jumping coach. And I checked on the horses in the afternoon. Bells seemed fine."

"Was there anyone else?"

Even though Will couldn't see her, she shook her head, then stopped. "Yeah. I asked Amos to put her in the round pen before Tori's lesson started."

Her pulse quickened. Their ranch foreman, Amos, had gone to jail for drug use in his early twenties. Since then, he'd worked at Lost Canyon Ranch and moved up from ranch hand to ranch foreman.

Her grip tightened on the cell phone. Grandpa

had trusted Amos completely. They'd established a strong friendship over the decades. And Amos had respected Grandpa. But did he respect *her*? If he didn't, would he be careless enough to use drugs and then come to work?

"I suggest you talk to Quinn and Amos and see what they have to say. Thankfully, Jingle Bells ingested a small amount that didn't hurt her permanently, but you wouldn't want this to happen again. Not only for the health of your horses but for anyone riding them."

"Of course."

"Also, given the circumstances, Tori will be taking lessons from one of the trainers at Serenity Stables."

"I understand. But Will?"

"Yeah?"

"Why did you want me to teach her lessons in the first place?"

He paused for a moment. "I'm surprised you have to ask. You're amazing with horses. Other than your grandpa, I've never seen anyone get through to them like you do."

"Oh." Warmth spread beneath her cheeks. That was kind of him to say. "I have to go. I need to talk to Amos. I'll see you around."

After ending the call, she quickly left Grandpa's room and strode outside. She had to get to the bottom of this.

Inside the barn, low grunts came from the hay loft. She stood at the bottom of the staircase. "Amos?"

"Up here."

Lainey took the stairs two at a time.

Amos bent over and picked up a square bale, stacking it above the rest. His hair—the color of wheat—lay matted to his forehead with a mixture of grease and sweat. He wiped his forehead with the back of his hand. "What do you need?"

"The vet just called. Jingle Bells had cocaine in her system on the day of the accident."

Amos picked up another bale and tossed it on the stack. His protruding belly hung over his belt buckle. "That's weird."

She put her hands on her hips. His nonchalant attitude grated on her nerves. "You aren't using again, are you?"

Amos spit a wad of chewing tobacco into an empty pop can. Anger flared in his steel-gray eyes. "How dare you. I've worked at Lost Canyon Ranch all this time, and that's how you treat me?"

She lifted her chin. "I was merely asking a question. A question I deserve an answer to."

His jaw twitched. "I haven't touched drugs in over thirty years." He turned his back to her and continued stacking the hay bales.

She gritted her teeth. "Did you see anyone else with Bells that day?"

"Nope."

A dull headache crept into her forehead. Was Amos lying? Had he relapsed? She'd have to keep a close eye on him. Despite his sour attitude, he was a hard worker, and it would be a shame to lose him.

She rubbed her temples. Grandpa would've known how to handle this.

———

Lainey brought her plate to the dining room table and sank down into the chair beside Quinn. Maximus squeezed in between their chairs, his nose resting by her thigh, waiting for table scraps. She barely noticed the border collie. Weariness hung over her like a heavy storm cloud.

What a week—Rebel was still refusing to eat and didn't want to leave the barn; Nutmeg was becoming restless, pacing in her stall, which was a sign that labor was near; Will was the permanent vet in Cherry Creek, so she'd have to see him on a regular basis; Quinn was completely shocked to hear what the vet had said, equally upset and unnerved that it had happened; and to top it off, Knox was still in town, snooping for information about her.

It couldn't get much worse.

At least Georgia had promised she'd keep an eye on Knox and tell Lainey what he was up to. That woman had quite the talent for keeping tabs on everyone in town. Might as well put it to good use.

Gripping a table knife, she cut into the marinated chicken breast Cheyenne had cooked for dinner. Her movements were sharp and jerky as she sliced the succulent meat into several pieces.

Quinn nudged her elbow. "You do realize the chicken is innocent, right?" She gave Lainey a sideways grin. "Next time, you're not getting a knife. You're scary with that thing."

"Very funny," she said dryly.

Cheyenne sat down across the table and poured a small amount of Italian dressing on a big plate of salad.

Strained silence filled the dining room, except for the clinks and clanks of silverware.

Lainey shifted in her chair. "Is Damian upset that you're stuck here for a month, Cheyenne?"

Her sister shrugged.

Lainey took a sip of cabernet and eyed Cheyenne over the rim of her wine glass. Her sister's reaction provoked more questions than answers. Damian was not only Cheyenne's boyfriend but also her music agent. He had to be angry that she wasn't in Nashville working. He had to be even more angry that she was in Cherry Creek. He didn't think very highly of

Lost Canyon Ranch. He'd made that quite clear when he'd visited two years ago and spent the entire visit boasting about his family's prestigious ranch in Tennessee.

"Are you doing any tours soon?" Quinn asked.

"Nothing's been planned. It's not like either of you would go to a concert anyway."

Lainey set down her wine glass. "When would we have time to take off and see a concert? The ranch won't run itself." She sucked in a breath the moment she'd spoken. It was the same excuse Grandpa had used for not resting after his first heart attack.

Her chest constricted. Maybe if she'd made him rest, he'd still be here.

The doorbell chimed.

"I'll get it." Lainey's chair skidded across the hardwood floor as she quickly rose from the table. She couldn't let her emotions get the best of her, not in front of her sisters. She had to be the strong one.

She walked through the kitchen and into the mudroom. Before she opened the door, she pulled back the curtains an inch.

An unfamiliar man wearing dress pants and a Canada Goose parka stood on the front porch. He shifted his weight from one foot to the other, then unzipped his coat to reach for something beneath.

She narrowed her eyes. Had Mt. Point Development sent another developer?

The man lifted his free hand to knock.

She yanked open the door. "I thought I'd made myself clear. I won't sell—"

"Are you Lainey Evans?" he asked.

"Um … yes."

The man thrust a long manila envelope at her. "You've been served." He turned and strode quickly to a parked Ford Contour that had the engine running.

She stood still for a moment, frozen in place. Her stomach coiled into a tight tangle of knots. She didn't have to look inside the envelope to read the details. Evelyn had decided to sue.

The week could get worse, after all.

Lainey trudged into the dining room and tossed the envelope at the end of the long wooden table. "I'm getting sued." Slumping into a chair, she rested her elbows on the table and put her head in her hands. "I never should've agreed to teaching Tori how to ride. What a mistake. Evelyn's hated me ever since I broke up with Will. She's probably happy the accident happened so she could finally get back at me."

Quinn shook her head. "You didn't realize it would turn out this way."

"I know, but now that it has, I'm screwed. Evelyn has a big mouth. The only reason the accident hasn't hit the gossip mill yet is because they're still in a tizzy about Cheyenne being in town," Lainey said. "They'll hear about it soon enough, though. How am I supposed to start a horse training business if people don't trust my training methods?"

"We'll figure something out." Quinn pushed mashed potatoes into a large clump on her plate before shoveling them into her mouth. "We won't let Evelyn take you down."

Lainey gave her sister a tentative smile. She straightened her posture and resumed eating. "Thanks, but the mayor's wife isn't our only problem. We need to decide what to do about Knox."

Cheyenne glanced at Quinn, then Lainey. Her gaze wavered to her plate and back up again. "Are you *sure* you don't want to hear what his offer is?"

Lainey dropped her fork, letting it clatter against her plate. "I'm positive. This is our home. This is where we grew up … together." She paused for a moment, letting her words sink in. "We can't just sell it to some developer who only cares about making money off of it."

Quinn nodded as she buttered a bun. "I agree. If Grandpa wanted to give it to us, then I don't want anyone else to have it."

Cheyenne finished her salad, chewing the last bite slowly. "But you could use the money to go to college, Quinn. Wouldn't that be amazing?"

Quinn scoffed. "Oh sure, go to college and never

use my degree, like you did? I still don't understand why you majored in business when you planned to become a singer. What a waste of Grandma and Grandpa's money."

Lainey's eyes widened. Whoa, where had that come from? Quinn was usually the peacekeeper.

Cheyenne ran her fingers through her long blond locks. "I got my degree so I'd have other options if singing didn't work out, which isn't a bad idea for you to consider as well. You can't compete forever."

Quinn tore off a piece of her bun and popped it into her mouth. "I'm at the peak of my training. My coach wants me to compete in the Denver Stock Show. Maybe that sounds stupid to a country music star, but to me, it's a big deal."

"Of course, it's a big deal. I'm proud of you." Cheyenne stood and picked up their plates. "I can never say the right thing when it comes to you two." She disappeared into the kitchen, returning a minute later with an apple pie. Steam rose from the top of the dessert as she set it on the table.

"Do you wish you were back in Nashville?" Quinn asked quietly.

Cheyenne cut into the dessert, dividing the slices and placing them onto small plates. "I'm surprised that Grandpa made such a ridiculous request, but I'm trying to make the best of it, and I'd like to help in any way I can."

Lainey bit into the pie. The taste of sweet cinnamon apples and warm flaky crust filled her mouth. She chewed slowly instead of responding. She had several retorts on the tip of her tongue, but none of them would produce a positive outcome.

Despite their harbored feelings, Grandpa wanted them to stick together, so she had to make an effort. And they needed to find a solution, as long as Cheyenne was on board. "If you really want to help, will you work with us to get rid of Knox?"

Cheyenne opened her mouth, then closed it. She tucked a strand of hair behind her ear. "Yes. But instead of getting rid of him, we should let him stay."

Lainey licked her fork and set it on her napkin. "Why would we do that?"

"Hear me out." Cheyenne straightened in her chair. "I found his company's website. Mt. Point Development became a Fortune 500 last year. If they want our land, they might be very persistent. Even if we get rid of Knox, his company could send someone else in his place."

"What are we supposed to do, then?" Quinn asked.

Cheyenne tapped a manicured finger against her chin. "Let him think we're interested in his offer, but tell him we need time to think about it."

Quinn perched on the edge of her chair. "That's

actually a great idea. It'll buy us time, and no one else will show up on our doorstep."

Lainey stared at her sisters. Didn't they see the one big flaw in this plan? "Um, Knox will. He'll keep showing up. And eventually, he'll want us to decide."

"You're right," Cheyenne said. "We'll need to make it believable that we're considering his offer."

Quinn nodded. "In the meantime, we should invite him to the ranch. Who knows, maybe he'll fall in love with it, and he won't want to buy it from us."

Lainey twisted loose strands of hair into a braid. "There's zero chance this guy will fall in love with the ranch. The sour look on his face when he walked into the barn … well, he could barely breathe." She almost smiled. The way his nose wrinkled had been kind of cute.

"You don't know him well enough to say there's zero chance." Quinn brushed her shoulder against Lainey's. "Plus, if anyone could make him see the value of our life here, it's you."

"Me? Now, wait a minute. I thought this was a team effort."

Quinn exchanged a knowing glance with Cheyenne. "It will be."

Lainey rose from the table. "I need to go check on Nutmeg and Rebel. But for the record, I don't like this plan."

"Hold on. While we're"—Cheyenne used air quotes—"*deciding* if we want to sell, we should also find out why his company wants the land. They probably want to build something. If we find out what it is, maybe we could show him why the ranch isn't the best spot for it."

Quinn smiled. "I was wrong. Your business degree *is* coming in handy."

Lainey rolled her eyes. Her sisters weren't thinking straight. Knox would see right through this plan.

But she had to admit, it was worth a try.

CHAPTER
Six

ON SATURDAY NIGHT, Knox parallel parked on Lumberjack Lane between a souped-up Chevy Silverado and a dirt-caked Jeep Wrangler. At the end of the street, a Road Closed sign blocked drivers from going any farther to make room for the parade.

A cold gust of wind blew in his direction as he walked toward downtown. Shivering, he lifted the collar of his gray wool coat. He needed to buy warmer clothes. This deal was taking much longer than he'd anticipated, and the wide-open spaces in Montana did little to block the brisk wind.

He turned onto Main Street, his eyebrows rising. Red suede bows were tied to the old-fashioned lamp posts. Decorated wreaths hung from the doors of each store. Tents were set up along the sidewalk with vendors selling a variety of products.

Wow. With the festive décor, Cherry Creek looked quite charming. This was the kind of event that out-of-town visitors would love. Not only would they enjoy the holiday decorations, but they'd be entertained by the townspeople.

Cherry Creek residents congregated on both sides of the street, bundled up in big puffy coats, thick gloves, and eccentric hats. One woman wore a hat shaped like a Christmas tree with battery-operated lights and ornaments. A large man holding a baby wore a plastic hat with reindeer antlers. Others had Santa hats with their names written on the front in glittery letters.

This town was unique, that was for sure. Knox stepped onto the sidewalk as a handful of kids ran by him, playing a game of tag.

A little boy bumped into him and stumbled backward. "Oops. Sorry."

He ruffled the boy's hair. "No problem, kiddo."

The boy sent Knox a toothy smile and jogged toward his friends.

He scrubbed a hand over his clean-shaven face. If he hadn't made work his first priority, would he already be married with kids by now?

Probably. As long as he'd met the right woman.

Not that he had regrets. He had a great plan in place. Work hard, gain a steady income, then get married and have a family. He wouldn't be the kind of husband or dad who was never around for his wife and kids.

"You need a hat." A plump woman stood outside her tent pointing to an array of cowboy hats and Christmas caps that hung from coatracks.

He stopped in front of her booth. So this was where people were buying the fun hats. "Will you help me pick one out?"

The vendor eyed him up and down, her cheeks reddening. She adjusted the straps on her overalls. "Certainly. Do any of them speak to you?"

He riffled through a few cowboy hats before picking up one made of straw.

"That's great for summer." She reached for a black wide-brimmed hat with silver trim. "Try this one. This here is a Montana Crease. It's made of felt and better suited for winter."

"OK." He handed her the straw hat and tried on the Montana Crease. He adjusted it over his hair and glanced at his reflection in a full-length mirror. What would Lainey think if she saw him wearing it? Would she find him less intimidating if he looked more like a cowboy and less like a businessman?

It was possible.

Knox handed the vendor cash. He tipped the front of the hat like he'd seen cowboys do in old Western movies. "Thank you."

She batted her eyelashes. "The pleasure was all mine."

Grinning, he strolled down the crowded sidewalk, scanning the crowd. It looked like everyone in Cherry Creek had shown up for the parade. He had to find Lainey. This would be the perfect opportunity to make a better impression on her.

Someone tapped on his shoulder. "Hey there."

He turned around at the sultry voice.

"I'm glad you're still in town." Scarlett loosened the fur scarf draped over her black coat. "I was afraid Georgia would scare you away."

"It would take a lot more than Georgia's mood swings to scare me off."

"A tough guy. I like that." She squeezed his arm affectionally before turning to the well-dressed couple standing nearby. "Knox, I'd like you to meet my mom and dad."

The man extended his hand and gave Knox's hand a firm shake. "Mr. Bennett. It's a pleasure to meet you in person. I'm Sam Sutherland, the mayor."

Knox pulled back his shoulders and lifted his chin. "Nice to meet you, Mr. Sutherland."

"Welcome to town. I'm Evelyn." Unlike her husband, the woman made no attempt to shake hands; instead, she touched the plastic brace circling her neck. "You'll have to excuse this horrible contraption. I was in a car accident in front of our neighbor's ranch. Lost Canyon Ranch, to be exact. One of their horses escaped and caused me to crash into a ditch." She paused for a moment, clearly waiting for him to respond. When he didn't, she continued, "I could've died."

Sam glanced at a family nearby who had stopped talking to overhear what Evelyn was saying. He wrapped his arm around his wife's lower back. "Now, Evie. It wasn't that bad."

"You weren't there, Sam." Evelyn pressed her palm against her ample chest. "It was terrible. My life flashed before my eyes."

"To make matters worse, my niece was there too," Scarlett added. "Now, Tori won't even go near a horse. That's why my mom is suing Lainey."

His lips parted. "Is that so?"

Evelyn leaned in close to his ear. "The sooner you own that property, the better."

"We should get going." Sam glanced up at the large clock tower at the center of town. "I have to start the parade. You let me know if you need anything, Mr. Bennett. Anything at all."

"Will do."

"I hope to see you again soon." Scarlett winked at him, then turned around, her hips swaying as she disappeared into the crowd with her parents.

Knox lifted the cowboy hat off his head and ran his fingers through his flattened hair. What the

Sutherlands had said was great news. Dealing with a lawsuit would give Lainey a reason to sell the ranch.

Ten minutes later, the first truck of the parade approached the corner of Main Street, letting out three honks. Sam stood on the back of the truck bed, holding a microphone. "Welcome to our thirty-third Blade Parade!"

Cherry Creek residents whooped and hollered.

"If you haven't met her yet, I'd like to introduce you to my granddaughter, Tori," the mayor said. "She'll start off the parade by singing 'I'll Be Home for Christmas.'"

A small redheaded girl with her arm in a cast took the microphone from Sam and began to sing.

"You have to be kidding me. They put Tori up there on purpose to show everyone she broke her arm."

Knox turned his head in the direction of Lainey's voice.

She stood a few feet away, talking to Quinn.

Perfect.

She must have felt his gaze because she turned in his direction.

Heat flushed beneath his cheeks when she didn't look away, and a light fluttering sensation traveled through his stomach. The reaction surprised him almost as much as the fact that she walked toward him.

"Got yourself a cowboy hat, huh?" She crossed her arms. "It's nice and all, but it's almost as if you're trying to fit in."

He smirked. "Did you just give me a compliment?"

She pressed her lips together as if holding back a retort.

"Is Cheyenne in the parade?" he asked. "Being that she's a celebrity, and all?"

"Not that I know of."

"How long will she be in Montana?"

Lainey put her hands on her hips. "If you have so many questions about Cheyenne, why don't you ask her? She's around here somewhere."

Was that a hint of jealousy in her tone? "I'm just making conversation. She *is* your sister."

Lainey sighed. "She's staying in town for a month. There. Are you happy?"

Yes, he was. As the only person interested in hearing his offer, Cheyenne would be more helpful the longer she stayed. If only Lainey would give him a chance. "I'm not a bad guy, you know."

She tapped a finger to her chin. "You want to take away my home, and you're telling me you're not a bad guy?"

Out on the street, Tori's voice rose as she held the last note of the song.

Knox moved closer to Lainey so she could hear

him. "I get it. Lost Canyon Ranch means a lot to you. But with the money I'm offering, you could buy a place with more land. You can have a bigger barn with more stalls, larger pens, and a house of your own."

"Wow, I really appreciate you figuring it all out for me." She didn't bother to hide the sarcasm in her tone.

Man, she was feisty. Under any other circumstances, he would find her sassiness sexy. But in this case, it only worked against him. "I don't want to fight with you. I want you to see that there are benefits to taking my offer. You would know if you'd just listen to it."

She leaned in toward him, their noses almost touching. "I'm not fighting *you*. I'm just doubting everything you say."

How was he supposed to respond? He couldn't think straight with her so close, the smell of soap and leather intoxicating his senses.

His heart hammered against his chest. Was it the argument or Lainey causing his heart to beat so quickly? Either way, he needed to get a grip. "I hate to tell you this, but I'm not going anywhere until you decide to sell."

She opened her mouth, then closed it. Indecision flickered in her eyes before she marched off into the crowd.

Damn. Knox squeezed the back of his neck. What would it take to convince Lainey to give up her home? No way was she completely content at that deteriorating ranch. There had to be something she wanted and would use the money for. It wasn't more land or a bigger barn. That was clear after talking to her tonight.

He had to find out what it was, and soon.

———

Lainey shifted from one foot to the other. Several trucks lumbered down Main Street behind the truck with the mayor. Each vehicle had a snowplow attached, decorated in different themes. One plow was covered in artificial snow with cardboard cutouts of Frosty the Snowman and kids dressed in winter wear. The next truck had a plow covered with aluminum foil to look like ice and people dressed up as Olaf, Anna, and Elsa in the truck bed.

It was hard to concentrate on the parade. Where were Cheyenne and Quinn? By the time she'd walked away from Knox, Quinn had moved to a different spot.

It wasn't just her sisters' whereabouts that had her unnerved. Knox wasn't visible either. She'd made it a block away before she'd changed her mind and gone back to talk to him. But he was nowhere near that corner of the street where she'd first seen him.

Ugh. Instead of playing nice and saying she would listen to his offer, she'd gotten upset. He was so infuriating. He wanted her to believe that he wasn't a bad guy? That he had good intentions?

She wasn't buying it.

Cheyenne maneuvered through the crowd carrying two Styrofoam cups. As she walked, several heads turned in her direction, but she didn't seem to notice. All the color had drained from her cheeks, giving her face a pale, ashen color.

"What's wrong?" Lainey asked.

Cheyenne looked over her shoulder. "Huh?"

"What's wrong?" she repeated.

"I thought I saw someone." Cheyenne swallowed. "You know what? Never mind. I think it was my imagination. It couldn't have been …" She handed one of the Styrofoam cups to Lainey. "I got you a hot chocolate. I hope you still like sprinkles and whipped cream on top."

"I do." She took a sip of the warm, frothy drink. Cheyenne was acting strange. Who had her sister *possibly* seen? Did she think someone was following her? A crazy fan, perhaps?

Cheyenne twisted the cup in her hands. "So, Quinn is sitting in a lawn chair next to Travis. I passed by them on my way over." Her brow furrowed. "What's going on between those two? She's not into him, is she?"

"Our ranch hand Travis?"

Cheyenne nodded.

"I don't think so. She hasn't said anything." Then again, Quinn *could* be interested in their ranch hand. Lainey had been so preoccupied with taking care of the ranch that she hadn't paid much attention to anything else.

"Sorry to interrupt." A teenage girl stood behind them, staring in awe at Cheyenne as she held out a napkin. "Could I get your autograph, Miss Evans?"

"Of course." Cheyenne smiled as she scribbled her signature. "There you go, darlin'."

The girl squealed. "Wow. I can't wait to show my friends. You know, Miss Evans, I went to your concert in Helena. You were amazing. Best. Concert. Ever."

Cheyenne tucked a strand of hair behind her ear. "I'm happy to hear that."

The girl clutched the signed napkin to her chest. "Thanks so much. Have a great night."

"You too, sweetie."

Lainey waited until the girl was far enough away that she couldn't overhear. "Does that ever get old?"

"No, not really. Most of the time, I enjoy it. I wouldn't have a career if I didn't have fans."

"I guess that's true." Lainey tried to focus her

attention on the parade again, but her mind was elsewhere. She and Cheyenne couldn't be more different. No one could pay her enough to stand on a stage in front of hundreds or thousands of fans. It was amazing that Cheyenne could thrive under that sort of pressure.

Heck, Lainey couldn't even handle the pressure of talking to Knox. That man frustrated her more than anyone else she'd ever met.

She stood on her tiptoes, scanning the crowd for him once again.

Still no sign of him. Pretty Boy should stick out like a sore thumb, even with that new cowboy hat. Heat crept up the back of her neck. The hat had looked really good on him.

Too good.

Annoyingly good.

She stopped the train of thought from going any further. Something was wrong with her. She shouldn't be thinking anything of the sort.

"Who are you looking for? Is there a boyfriend I haven't heard about yet?" Cheyenne asked.

Lainey shook her head. "Definitely not. The dating pool in Cherry Creek is about as shallow as it ever was. I was hoping I'd run into Knox. I need to put our plan into action." She wouldn't mention that she'd already had a chance and royally messed it up.

"I haven't seen him." Cheyenne's phone rang to

the tune of Reba McEntire's "Consider Me Gone." She quickly silenced the call and stuffed the phone into her pocket. "It looks like everyone has scooted closer to the curb, so you'd have a straight shot if you took the sidewalk. You'd have to see him as long as he's on this side of the street."

"That's true. I'll be back before the parade is over." Lainey finished the last few drops of her hot chocolate and threw the cup away in the nearest trash can. Whose call was Cheyenne ignoring?

She glanced back at her sister. Cheyenne had the phone up to one ear, her hand cupping the other ear to drown out the noise.

It must be her boyfriend.

Disgust rose like bile in Lainey's throat. What did Cheyenne see in Damian Hart? The one and only time he'd visited Lost Canyon Ranch, he'd been smug. Conceited. Full of himself. She could go on and on. When it came down to it, he wasn't good enough for her sister.

Lainey stuffed her hands in the front pockets of her leather coat and shook off all thoughts of Damian. She forced her feet to walk slowly. Casual. As if she wasn't nervous to talk to Knox. She had a higher chance of putting her foot in her mouth than having the right words come out of it.

A minute later, she found him.

Knox stood in front of the Wagon Wheel Café,

having a conversation with Georgia. He leaned against the brick building, ankles crossed and a wide grin on his face.

What a charming smile he had. She shook her head. Probably got him far in life, schmoozing people to get what he wanted.

Taking a deep breath, she headed his way. As she moved closer, he looked in her direction. His grin wavered, but he kept it plastered on his all-too-handsome face.

"Are you enjoying the parade?" she asked politely.

"I am. It's very unique with all the snowplows decorated. Now I understand why it's called the Blade Parade."

Georgia swiped her palms back and forth, like she was trying to light a fire. "My favorite one was the Grinch-themed truck. But that guy in the Grinch costume looked real. He gave me the heebie-jeebies."

Lainey put a hand on the older woman's shoulder. "Don't worry, Georgia. No one will mess with you. We all know you sleep with a loaded pink pistol next to your bed."

Georgia's eyes grew as round as saucers. "How'd you know that?"

"Because you've told me. Numerous times."

"Oh." Georgia's brow wrinkled in thought, then smoothed out when she looked at Knox and pointed a finger at him. "One can never be too careful around here. You never know who could be out to get you."

Lainey resisted the urge to laugh. This town might have vicious gossip, but danger? No. "Um, Georgia? Could I talk to Knox alone, please?"

Georgia's gaze darted from Knox to Lainey. She zipped her sparkly fuchsia coat up to her collarbone. "I'm hungry. I think I'll go fetch myself some of those delicious-looking gingerbread cookies."

Lainey gave Georgia a grateful smile and looked fully at Knox—the dimple in his chin, his long dark eyelashes, his deep-set eyes. Her breath caught in her throat. Why did he have to be so attractive? "I was too harsh earlier. I'm sorry."

"It's OK. I understand where you're coming from." His response sounded forced, like he was trying to keep his voice steady, but he couldn't hide the surprise in his tone.

Ha. She had to revel in catching him off guard. And yet, anxious adrenaline still coursed through her veins. "My sisters and I will listen to your offer."

He rocked back on his heels, his face stoic. "That's wonderful."

His casual composure was so darn unnerving. "Don't expect us to make a decision right away, though. We'll need time to consider our options."

"Of course. It's a big decision."

She fidgeted with the sleeves of her coat. This was

such a bad idea. And yet, if her sisters were right, they'd buy themselves some time. Not that she had any hope of their success, but if they stalled long enough, maybe Mt. Point Development would give up. "Would you like to go on a trail ride with me tomorrow afternoon at two? Afterward, you can stay for dinner and present your offer to us."

"A trail ride?"

"Yup. Horseback riding."

"Oh. Yeah, sure." A mixture of emotions crossed his face—uncertainty, fear, followed by relief. He was clearly afraid to ride, but it must be setting in that she'd given him the opportunity to present his offer. "That sounds … perfect."

Lainey chewed on the inside of her cheek. Knox looked so hopeful she almost felt guilty.

Almost.

CHAPTER
Seven

TURNING INTO LOST CANYON RANCH, Knox eased his foot off the gas pedal and slowly drove his truck up the long, winding driveway. The horses to his left glanced up as he passed by. To the right, plump cows grazed on the grass, paying little attention to his vehicle.

Knox gripped the steering wheel and took a deep breath. This was it. The moment he'd been waiting for. An opportunity to share Mt. Point Development's offer.

He'd prepared good reasons for Cheyenne and Quinn to give up the ranch. He had Georgia to thank for that. That woman sure could talk. At the Blade Parade, he'd learned a great deal about the two women.

This time, he wasn't just throwing money in their direction. It would be personal.

Unfortunately, he hadn't discovered what Lainey would use the extra money for. He'd have to try to get it out of her today during the trail ride.

As he parked, she stepped out of the cabin, wearing faded jeans and a thick green coat. Her hair was tied in a low ponytail that fell in soft waves over her shoulder. She didn't have any makeup on—not that she needed any—she had a naturally pink hue in her cheeks, and her bright blue eyes were stunning all on their own.

"Ready?" she asked.

"As I'll ever be."

A brown-and-white border collie dashed off the porch to come sniff the bottom of Knox's shoes. He leaned over and scratched behind the dog's ears. "Who's this?"

"Maximus. He'll be coming with us on the trail."

"So, you have a dog, cattle, and horses. Do you have any other animals?"

"Chickens. There's a coop behind the house. We also have cats. They run around the ranch, taking shelter in our garage or the barn. We don't let them in the house. We mainly keep them so they'll chase away the mice."

He stiffened. "Mice?"

A playful smile spread across her face. "You aren't afraid of mice, are you?"

He puffed out his chest. "No, of course not."

"I don't believe you."

He blew out a breath and lowered his shoulders. "Fine. Maybe a little."

"That's what I thought." Lainey smirked, not in a taunting way, but in a "I'm glad I broke through your manly façade" kind of way. "Follow me." As she moved toward the barn, she gave him a thorough once-over.

He patted his wool coat in several spots. "What? Did I spill something?"

"No need to worry, Mr. Hot Shot, you don't have any stains."

"Good." Wait. Did she call him Mr. Hot Shot? Was that really what she thought of him?

"Actually, I was thinking I should've told you to bring boots and a warmer coat. It gets pretty cold on the trails, especially once we move into the woods. But Grandpa's clothes might fit you. What size shoe do you wear?"

"Eleven and a half."

"Grandpa wore a size twelve. His boots might be a little big on you, but that's better than being too small."

"OK." He followed her toward the barn. He

stepped inside and resisted the urge to gag. Hints of sweaty leather, urine, and horse manure filled the air. Small equipment and rusted tools lay haphazardly on mismatched shelves and benches. How could Lainey or anyone else function in a space this unorganized?

She met his gaze and shrugged. "I don't have a lot of time to clean anything in here besides the horse's stalls."

His cheeks flushed. How had she known what he was thinking? Either she was good at reading him, or he wasn't as good at hiding his reactions as he'd thought.

She bent over a pile of boots, her jeans stretching tightly over her hips. "Here, try these on."

Heat pooled low in his stomach. Those jeans fit her in all the right places. He swallowed hard and averted his gaze as he moved an empty bucket off the nearest bench, so he could sit down. He took off his tennis shoes, then tugged on the boots. Paul McKinley's feet might have been longer, but Knox's feet were wider. Or were all cowboy boots supposed to fit this snugly? He'd never worn them before.

"Well?" Lainey asked.

"They'll work." He stood and draped his jacket across an empty stall.

She handed him a hooded Carhartt work coat.

For a brief moment, their hands touched, sending tingles down his spine. He pulled his hand away quickly and slipped his arms inside the coat. The sleeves were the right length, and it fit fairly well over his shoulders, albeit a little snug. "This is much warmer than mine. Thanks."

"Glad it fits," she said quietly.

She blinked, then blinked again, lowering the tip of her brown cowgirl hat.

Were there tears in her eyes? An unexpected ache squeezed inside his chest. He unzipped the coat. "I don't have to wear this. I don't mind being cold."

"No," she said quickly. "It's fine."

He opened his mouth to tell her that she didn't have to be so brave, that it was perfectly acceptable to grieve. But before he could get the words out, a black-and-white horse poked his head out of a nearby stall. *Oh no.* It looked like the same one that had slobbered all over his suit.

The animal extended its neck before Knox could take a step back, and nuzzled its nose against Knox's chest. He tried not to breathe as the animal sniffed Paul McKinley's coat. A soft pleasing neigh escaped from its throat.

Lainey's mouth hung open. "No way."

"What?" Knox moved back farther.

"I can't believe it." Her chest rose and fell. "Don't move."

"OK …" He stayed put, stiff and rigid. What was going on?

She disappeared into a room at the back of the barn and came back a minute later with a bucket. "Try feeding this to Rebel."

Knox lowered the bucket over the stall door, holding on to the handle.

Rebel sniffed Paul's coat again. His ears perked.

Lainey gripped the top of the stall door and stared at the horse. "Come on, Rebel. Eat, buddy. You've got to be hungry."

The horse lowered his muzzle into the pail. When his head popped back up, he was chewing.

A wide grin spread across her face, showcasing her perfect white teeth. "Why didn't I think of this before? He likes the smell of Grandpa's clothes." Joy lit in her big blue eyes. "It's making him happy enough to eat."

With Lainey's undivided attention on the horse, Knox shifted his weight from one boot to the other. This was a first—becoming a third wheel when he was the only other human in the room with a woman.

After a few more minutes, she tore her gaze away to look at Knox. "Sorry to get all weird on you. Rebel was my grandpa's horse." As she spoke, she stroked the horse's mane. "I've been really worried about him. He's been depressed ever since … well, you know."

She turned back to Rebel. "Would you like to go

for a trail ride, boy? I'm sure your new friend would love to ride you."

The horse moved his head up and down.

"Did the horse just nod, or am I going crazy?"

A slow smile spread across her face. "Yes. Horses are considered one of the most intelligent animals on earth."

"I didn't know that."

"Want to know something else?"

"Yes," he said, transfixed by her excitement.

"In the wild, horses will synchronize their heartbeats to other horses in the herd in order to sense danger more quickly. Many domesticated horses will do the same with humans. So, while you're riding, pay attention to your heartbeat. You'll probably notice that it changes. It can be a very calming experience."

"Is that why horses are used for therapy?"

"Yup. They're the perfect animals for any rehabilitation because they have that special ability to calm people down."

"That's really cool."

"It is, isn't it?" Lainey beamed.

He'd never seen her in such a good mood. This could only help his chances tonight at dinner.

Twenty minutes later, Knox rode Rebel, and Lainey rode her palomino, Jingle Bells. The wide trail wove through the woodlands, heading up the mountains. Maximus ran ahead, nose to the ground, disappearing and reappearing as he followed scents. Birds flitted above, flying from thick Douglas firs to tall lodgepole pines.

He inhaled the fresh mountain air, trying to relax. Time to get to know Lainey and see if she'd open up to him. "How did your horse get the name Jingle Bells?"

A faraway look clouded her eyes. "Grandpa bought her for me for Christmas when I was sixteen. He had a big bow with bells wrapped around her neck, and every time she moved, the bells jingled."

Knox smiled. "Very fitting, then." He shifted his position on the saddle as Rebel slowed significantly. His thighs were already sore. "Why's he going so slow?"

"Because he's pooping."

"He can move and … uh, do his business at the same time?"

She giggled. "You really don't know a lot about horses, do you?"

"No." At least she found his inexperience funny. Not only because he needed her to be in a good mood later but because his heart did an unexpected flutter when she laughed.

He swallowed hard and turned his attention to their surroundings. Thin rays of sunlight broke through the gaps in the trees, casting light on a dark shack sandwiched between two large junipers. "What's that?"

She followed his gaze. "My grandpa used it as a hunting cabin. He'd stay there so he could wake up early or stay up late and hunt in the surrounding area. It hasn't been used in over a decade. When we started expanding the herd, he didn't have much time to hunt. Cattle are a lot of work. Plus, it's haunted."

Knox peered through the thick brush as Maximus trotted back, walking slightly in front of the horses to lead the way. "You don't seriously believe that, do you?"

A mysterious glint sparked in her eyes. "There's a story behind the haunting. Do you want to hear it?"

"Sure. But I don't believe in ghosts."

"Yet." She grinned. "The story begins in 1910 with the Yates family. There was a dad, a mom, four sons, and a daughter. Like a lot of people in those days, they came from Europe and landed at Ellis Island, New York. Once they got to America, they needed a place to live. At the time, the government had a deal called the Homestead Act." She paused to look at him. "Do you know what that is?"

"That's when the government gave people a piece of land for free if they lived on it and cultivated it. Right?"

"Exactly. So, the Yateses decided to move out west

to Cherry Creek. There was a small settlement with a few stores, a claims office, and not much else. The Yateses realized how good the soil was, saw the potential for living near the mountains and the creeks, and decided to lay down their roots."

"Sounds like they made a good choice."

"Why don't you wait until the end to make that conclusion?" She took a breath before continuing. "Winters were hard. Lots of snow. People went stir-crazy, some starved to death. During their first winter on the land, the oldest son, Henry, offered to travel to town to get food. It was a huge risk. It took two days to travel there and back by horse. He could've gotten stuck in the storm, or been attacked by other pioneers, natives, or wild animals."

"Brave kid. What happened to him?"

"Henry was fine. He did get stuck in the storm, and it took three days instead of two to get back home, but he made it." She paused for a moment. "Unfortunately, his family didn't have the same fate. When Henry arrived home, there wasn't any smoke coming out of the fireplace. No smoke was a bad sign. Back then, people needed a fire to cook and stay warm. Henry ran into the house, yelling for his family, and discovered everyone had been beheaded, except for his little sister, Olivia."

"Wow." This was probably an imaginary tale passed down from generation to generation, but he would appease Lainey anyway. "So, how did Olivia escape the murderers?"

"Are you sure you want to know? I wouldn't want to give you nightmares."

He put a hand to his chest. "Thanks for your concern, but you can't leave me hanging."

"Fine, but don't blame me when you can't sleep tonight."

"I'll be all right. I don't get scared easily."

"If you say so." When she continued, she spoke quieter. "Henry found his sister in the loft, sitting in a rocking chair. When he walked closer to her, he spotted a shiny piece of jewelry on the floor. It was his mother's necklace, the one she always wore and never took off. He bent down to pick it up when …" Lainey clapped her hands together. "Whack! Olivia cut off Henry's head."

A cold gust of wind blew in their direction. Knox shivered and quickly gave Lainey a knowing look. "I'm cold, not scared."

"Sure," she said, looking unconvinced. "Neighbors came to see the family and found all the bodies, but they couldn't find Olivia. She was nowhere to be seen. Some said they saw a light appear in the windows, but there was no physical evidence that a person was still living there. For years, no one wanted to buy land where people were murdered, but eventually, my great-grandfather did. Because of the location and the girl, he decided to name the property Lost Canyon Ranch."

"That's quite the story," Knox said.

Bad winters were realistic. An entire family being murdered could've happened. But a ghost haunting the cabin? Nope. Not possible. Lainey probably didn't believe it either, she was just trying to scare him.

She wagged a finger in his direction. "Before you try to disprove my story, let me tell you this … When I was a teenager, my sisters and I camped in a tent near the shack. It was late, we were getting ready to go to sleep when we saw a flicker of light, as if someone had lit a candle."

"Did you go inside to make *sure* no one was there?" he asked.

"Heck no. We screamed and ran all the way home."

She laughed—a light airy sound that made the tension in his shoulders loosen. Or maybe it was Rebel's doing, synchronizing their heartbeats.

"We'll head a little higher up the mountain before we turn around."

"Sounds good." Knox took one last glance at the shack. The outline of a face appeared behind one of the dusty windows.

Huh? He squeezed his eyes shut, then opened

them. The face was gone. No one was there. He shook his head. He'd only imagined it, right?

A shiver ran down his spine.

What was wrong with him? He needed to stay focused on more realistic issues—like making an appealing offer to Lainey, Cheyenne, and Quinn at dinner. He still hadn't discovered a good reason for Lainey to sell, but he'd have to try without it.

If all went well, the three of them would be open-minded about selling the ranch. They'd be able to set aside their emotions and see the offer for what it was —a fresh start to a better life. That was how he saw it. The question was, would they?

———

Lainey reached for a napkin to wipe lasagna sauce off her lips. Her hand brushed against Knox's forearm, and they locked eyes. Her stomach did an airy somersault. *Look away, Lainey. He's the enemy.* She glanced down at her plate, mentally chastising herself. What was she doing? Sure, he was good-looking. But still. He was trying to take away her home.

She had to admit, she *did* enjoy the trail ride with him this afternoon. It was refreshing to talk to someone who hadn't lived in Cherry Creek his whole life. Retelling the ghost story was fun, especially since she didn't actually believe the shack was haunted. She had seen the candlelight as a teenager, though, which was weird. Knox must've thought so too because, for a moment, it looked as if he'd been scared. It was kind of cute.

As soon as they'd arrived at the ranch and untacked the horses, a heavy weight had again pressed against her chest. Knox was here for one reason and one reason only—to obtain the land for his company. Just like her and her sisters, he most likely had a plan to achieve his goal.

She crumpled the napkin with a tight grip. Would he lure Cheyenne into believing whatever he said? Lainey couldn't let that happen.

Knox finished the last of his lasagna and cleared his throat. "That was delicious, Cheyenne. Thank you."

"You're welcome." Her sister's response came out sharp and fast.

Lainey eyed Cheyenne across the table and shifted in her chair. Why was her sister so tense? Hopefully not because she'd already had a change of heart about stalling Knox.

If only they were open with one another like they'd been as kids. For many years, the three of them had shared a bedroom. They stayed up late into the night, talking about school, boys, and rodeos. They would jump into Lainey's bed, giggling quietly under the sheets.

But then Cheyenne started singing in a local band, staying out late to play gigs, and she'd asked Grandpa if she could have the loft to herself. That request had been the beginning of their rift.

Knox moved his empty plate aside. "I don't want to keep you up too late, so it's best if I get started." He reached for his briefcase sitting beside his chair and opened it on his lap. Papers were filed into neat stacks with clips.

He took three papers off the top pile and handed each of them a copy. "As you know, Mt. Point Development is interested in acquiring Lost Canyon Ranch. The property is currently valued at two million five hundred thousand dollars." He gave his most charming smile, showcasing the dimple in his chin. "We'd like to buy it from you for three million."

She choked on her own saliva. Three million dollars? He wanted to give them five hundred thousand over the property value. Was he insane? Why would his company do that?

The glass in Cheyenne's hand shook. Drops of wine spilled onto her fingers.

Quinn sat rigidly still, her eyebrows rising so high they disappeared beneath her bangs.

Lainey turned in her chair so she could face him directly. "That's a lot of money to shell out for a ranch in the middle of nowhere Montana. What's in it for your company?"

"It's the biggest property in Cherry Creek. You can see five different mountain ranges from your house. It's got easy access to hiking trails. It doesn't get as much snow as other areas of Montana. It's on the edge of town, so it's right off the interstate for travelers. All in all, it's a great location."

"Why are you interested in travelers?" Quinn asked.

His Adam's apple bobbed up and down, but his body language remained calm and confident. "We'd like to build a dude ranch resort."

Lainey bit down hard on her tongue. "Ouch." Ignoring the sting, she shook her head. "You can't build a resort on this ranch. My great-grandfather …"

Cheyenne kicked her under the table.

"Never mind. Continue," she mumbled.

"We're offering more money than the property value because we understand the sacrifice we're asking you to make." Knox rested his elbows on the table and gestured with his hands. "This money could benefit each of you. Cheyenne, if you sell the ranch, you'll have no more responsibilities keeping you in Cherry Creek. You'd be free to go back to Nashville."

Nervous adrenaline shot through Lainey's limbs.

She crossed one leg over the other, then uncrossed them. It was *so* hard to sit still.

"Quinn, I've been told you're a talented show jumper. Think about what you could do with the extra money. You could buy a new horse to compete with. You could even buy your own practice equipment."

Quinn pursed her lips, but her eyes were telling—she was considering what Knox said.

Lainey moved both feet to the floor and drummed her short fingernails on the wooden table. This wasn't good. Quinn was supposed to be on *her* side.

Knox put his hand over Lainey's. "I know this place means a lot to you. It's hard to see it as anything but your home, but the land has a lot of potential. It could be a relaxing getaway. Couples could hike together or go horseback riding through the mountains. A resort in"—he paused to use air quotes—"*nowhere* Montana would be the perfect location for families to spend time together, for kids to enjoy being outdoors, or for couples to reunite."

She resisted the urge to remove his hand from hers. His touch felt too comfortable, too intimate to match the heartless words coming out of his mouth. It was clear that he held a very different perspective from hers. He saw the offer as an overly nice gesture with a dollar sign attached to it. He viewed it as a business deal where he could build something new, to create a place where families could make memories. He didn't realize that in doing so, he would also take away their family home and the legacy that Grandpa had bestowed to them. He didn't see her viewpoint at all.

But he would. She would make sure of it.

Knox shut his briefcase. "I know you said you need time to consider my offer, so if you have any questions at all, please feel free to reach out to me." He set a business card on the table. "My cell phone number is on here, and I also added the number to my hotel room in Red Lodge."

"You're not staying in Cherry Creek?" Cheyenne asked.

"I was, but the Lucky Motel closed."

Quinn wrinkled her nose. "I don't know how that place stayed in business for as long as it did. They had a lot of drug-related activity going on. The police were called multiple times."

Cheyenne toyed with her earring. "Would you … Do you want to stay with us?"

Lainey glared at her sister. She did *not* just suggest Knox stay at their house.

He looked as surprised as she did, his eyes widening to the size of Roma tomatoes. "That's kind of you to offer, but I couldn't impose on you like that."

Clip-clop. Clip-clop. Clip-clop.

Lainey exchanged a look of confusion with Quinn. That sounded like a horse, but her sister had put all the horses in their stalls for the night.

Clip-clop. Clip-clop. Clip-clop.

Rebel peeked in the dining room window. His black-and-white ears perked as soon as he caught sight of Knox. He let out a neigh.

Knox laughed. "I guess I made quite the impression on Rebel, huh?"

Lainey rolled her eyes, but deep down, relief washed through her. Rebel was fond of Knox. The only reason the Appaloosa had eaten and gone on a trail ride was because of the developer.

"How in the world did Rebel get out?" Cheyenne asked.

Quinn put her hands up in innocence. "I promise I shut the latch."

"Rebel is one of the smartest horses we have," Lainey said. "He must've learned how to unlock the latch. This is a good sign. He's becoming his old ornery self again."

"I'll go put him in the barn." Quinn rose from the table. "Be right back."

Silence settled over the room in her sister's absence, giving Lainey time to think. Maybe Knox staying here wasn't such a bad idea. If he stayed at the ranch, he'd see Rebel more often. This might be exactly what the horse needed to get back on track. Of course, the horse would be upset when Knox eventually left, but it wouldn't be as hard on him as losing Grandpa.

When Quinn returned, Lainey sat up straighter in her chair. "You wouldn't be imposing, Knox. And this way, you won't have to drive on bad roads. I could smell snow coming when we were in the mountains today. It's teasing the air."

Cheyenne's lips parted as if she was processing the fact that Lainey had agreed with her. "You could stay in the loft. I'll move downstairs into my mom's room. You'll have more space and privacy up there."

Knox ran a hand through his hair. "It wouldn't feel right unless I paid you rent."

Cheyenne shook her head.

"I insist. I get reimbursed for all my travel expenses, anyway."

"OK," Lainey said. "Feel free to bring your stuff over tomorrow, then." She chewed on the inside of her cheek. It wouldn't be easy having him around, constantly in their business. But she would do anything to get Rebel back to his old self. He was all she had left of Grandpa.

CHAPTER
Eight

ON MONDAY, Knox left the hotel in Red Lodge. Heavy clouds hung low in the sky as he headed straight for the Wagon Wheel Café. He needed to call Vince and get some work done on his other projects before he took up residence at Lost Canyon Ranch.

The café would have faster internet, better cell service, and coffee. He needed all the caffeine he could get. Last night, he'd woken up to a nightmare about a ghost chasing him through the woods.

The face he'd seen in the window had looked very real.

But it couldn't have been.

No way would he tell Lainey. She'd think he was a wuss.

After the nightmare, it had taken a while to fall back asleep. He'd tossed and turned, thinking about

Lainey and her sisters. They were up to something. Maybe a "keep your friends close and your enemies closer" kind of deal.

Whatever their motives were, he'd agreed. It was the most unorthodox decision he'd ever made in order to obtain a property. But the more time he spent with Lainey, the better chances he had of figuring out what she would use the money on.

All in all, he was one step closer to getting the deal done.

One step closer to becoming vice president of Mt. Point Development.

The Wagon Wheel Café was bustling with noise. Georgia flitted over to his booth as soon as he sat down. She had a full coffeepot in one hand and packets of creamer in the other.

"You're the best," he said, setting his work tablet on the table.

"Anything for you, Hot Cakes." She shook her head and mumbled to herself. "No, that's not it either." She looked up as if the answer were written on the ceiling. "How about Hot Sauce? Nope. Hot Tamale? No."

He took a sip of coffee as soon as she poured it. "You could just call me Knox."

Georgia put a hand on her bony hip. "I should think not. I don't call anyone by their given name. It'll come to me when the time is right. Don't you worry." Without another word, she left to refill coffee at a nearby table where two gray-haired men sat eating breakfast. One of the men was tall and lanky and was wearing a suit, while the other was short and stocky, wearing a brown sheriff's uniform.

The lanky man took a bite of hash browns, then pointed his empty fork at the sheriff. "I hate to tell you this, Hank, but you look like a raccoon with those bags under your eyes."

Scowling, Hank leaned forward and rested his elbows on the table. "Another late night at the Outlaw Saloon. Had to arrest five men. All of them had drugs in their system."

"Cocaine again?"

The sheriff nodded.

"Where is it coming from?"

Hank scrubbed a hand over the stubble on his face. "Dunno, Floyd. Wish I did. The sheriff's department is doing everything we can to find out."

Knox frowned. More trouble? Cherry Creek could go downhill fast if the sheriff couldn't get to the bottom of the illegal activity. That would be a shame. After attending the Blade Parade, it was obvious how much the citizens loved this town.

Unfortunately, it was only obvious because of the people. The state of downtown said otherwise.

He glanced out the window. Across the street, Bulls and Barbers had a chunk of cement broken off their front step. The thrift shop, Finders Keepers, had a huge tear through their awning.

He turned on his tablet, created a new folder, and labeled it: Ideas for Downtown Cherry Creek. If it were up to him, he'd capitalize on the beautiful backdrop of the mountains by adding rustic cabin décor all along the street—black bear statues, wooden barrels with flower-pots, handcrafted benches, old-fashioned lantern lights.

A good start. Maybe he could run it by the mayor after the resort was taken care of. He'd send someone else from Mt. Point Development to do it because he'd be busy acclimating to his new role. Hopefully.

He clicked on the folder for Lost Canyon Ranch and called Boss Man.

Vince answered on the fifth ring. "Hey, Knox. Sorry, I almost missed you. I was in a meeting with Tyler Hansen. He's wrapping up a project in Belle-vue, Washington."

"A brewery, right?"

"Yes. It's called Paws and Pints." Vince chuckled. "Apparently, allowing pets at breweries is a new incentive for patrons."

"Interesting." Knox shifted in the booth. It sounded liked Tyler's project was going well. Which was good for the company. But Knox didn't exactly feel great about it. Tyler might be one of the people Vince was considering as a replacement.

"Any progress with McKinley's granddaughters?" Vince asked.

He sat up straighter. "Yes, I presented the offer to them last night. Two out of the three women seem interested in selling."

"*Seem* interested? We gave them a great offer."

"Their emotional attachment to the ranch is clouding their judgment."

"That's disappointing. Our client is getting anxious and would like the deal to go through soon. As you can imagine, the money that G. S. put down for a retainer fee is dwindling away quickly, and quite frankly, you have nothing to show for it."

Knox raked a hand through his hair. If only he knew who the anonymous client was. Whoever it was, they were hiding their identity for a reason. Was G. S. a family friend who didn't want to create strife between them? The only person he'd met whose name started with a *G* was Georgia. She already owned the café, though, so why would she want to open a resort?

There were also plenty of people who could have *G* names that he hadn't met yet.

Or was the client a relative of Lainey's who didn't want to cause family drama? Cheyenne had seemed eager to listen to his offer. Could she possibly be the client and had created the initials to cover up her identity? And what about their mom and dad? Where were they?

There were too many possibilities at this point. But one thing was certain—G. S. was watching Knox's every move.

He scanned the café. Unlike the attention he'd first received after arriving in Cherry Creek, no one was looking in his direction. Hank and Floyd had left. A younger couple had taken their table, their gazes fixed on one another.

Vince cleared his throat. "Knox?"

"Yes, sir?"

"Keep working on the granddaughters. Do whatever you need to do to get that land."

———

Later that afternoon, Lainey kicked off her boots in the mudroom. Snow slid off her clothes as she took off layers of clothing. This morning, the weather had started off with a light snowfall, and within a few hours, they'd ended up with four inches on the ground. Compared to other areas of Montana, they didn't get a lot of snow. The air was too dry to hold much moisture. But every now and then, a big winter snowstorm would hit.

No matter how many inches fell, if the snow didn't melt right away, something needed to be done about it. With Amos and Travis living in trailers on the property, they'd quickly plowed paths to and from the paddocks, the barn, the garage, and the driveway.

In the meantime, she'd collected eggs from the henhouse, chopped wood for kindling, and given the horses new bedding, water, and fresh oats. She'd put most of the horses out to pasture while she worked in their stalls, but Nutmeg had refused to leave. Lainey had to work around the horse while the mare paced back and forth.

After cleaning the stall, Lainey had examined Nutmeg, discovering her udders were filling in with milk. Labor was near.

Shedding her last layer of clothes except for her jeans and sweatshirt, Lainey headed toward the kitchen. Would she be able to save the mare and the premature foal? If Grandpa were here, she wouldn't be as nervous. He always knew what to do.

Too bad Quinn couldn't help, but her sister had left early to train.

Lainey would have to do it on her own.

Inside the kitchen, the smell of chili and corn bread filled the room.

"Hey there." Cheyenne opened the oven, pulled out a pan of corn bread, and set it on the faded countertop.

"Thanks for making lunch." Lainey filled a bowl

with chili and sat down at the table. She had to admit, it was nice having Cheyenne around to cook. Between Lainey's responsibilities on the ranch and Quinn's training schedule, there was no way they'd be eating any meals if it weren't for Cheyenne.

She dipped her spoon into the chili, her gaze traveling toward the staircase. What was Knox doing in the loft? He'd arrived over an hour ago. Was he avoiding them? Worst case scenario, he was inspecting his room and trying to find something wrong with it. Electrical outlets. Uneven flooring. Mold. Who knew what kind of expertise he had working for a development company?

And if he found something wrong, he'd surely use it to his advantage. She could already hear him … *Did you realize the house has severe foundation issues? It'll cost twenty thousand dollars to fix. But don't worry, you won't need to fix it if you sell the land to me.*

Maybe offering for him to stay had been a bad idea. Just as bad as Cheyenne's plan to string him along until they were forced to come clean and tell him they weren't selling. Hopefully, it was worth the trouble of keeping Knox around so he could help Rebel adjust to Grandpa's absence.

Cheyenne tugged a rooster-themed oven mitt off her hand before turning off the oven and taking a seat beside Lainey. "You look exhausted."

"I'll sleep in January when things calm down a little."

"I'm worried about you. You're up before anyone else in the morning, and you spend most of your nights in the office."

Lainey shrugged. Since when did Cheyenne care enough to be worried about her? "Someone's gotta do it."

Cheyenne set her hand on Lainey's forearm. "Let me help. What can I do to lighten your load?"

"You're cooking meals three times a day. I'd say that's enough."

Cheyenne shook her head. "What is something Mom did that I could do instead?"

Lainey stood and cut into the warm corn bread, bringing a piece back to the table. "You could check the henhouse for eggs in the mornings."

"OK." Cheyenne nibbled on her bottom lip—her telltale sign that she had more to say and wasn't sure if she should.

Lainey drizzled honey over the bread. "What is it? You might as well get it off your chest."

"I don't want you to take this the wrong way, but I think you'd be a lot happier if you went out once in a while. Maybe go to a movie or the mall or go get a pedicure."

She scowled. "A pedicure? Why the heck would I do that when my feet are in boots all day?"

A look of bewilderment crossed Cheyenne's delicate features. "It's relaxing. It would give you a short break. And if anyone needs more breaks, it's you."

"Having a stranger rub my feet sounds anything but relaxing."

Cheyenne walked to the sink and filled it with soapy water. "I'm trying to help you, but of course, your first instinct is to disagree with me." She moved the corn bread into a Tupperware container, then scrubbed the empty pan with unnecessary force. "Ever since I moved to Nashville, it's never been the same between us."

Lainey sighed. "That's because you never told me you wanted to go. One day, you packed up all your things and left. You didn't even bother to say goodbye."

Cheyenne stopped scrubbing. "I didn't?"

"No."

"It wasn't on purpose. I—"

Heavy footfalls thumped down the stairs. Lainey frowned. Just great. Knox had overheard their private conversation. He'd probably try to use it to his benefit somehow.

Seconds later, he ambled into the kitchen. His hair was disheveled and jutted out at odd angles. Lines creased his right cheek from where he must have lain on his pillow.

For the first time since he'd arrived in Cherry

Creek, Knox looked … normal. Comfortable. Not so business-like.

Flutters took flight inside her stomach, replacing the flare of frustration that had simmered moments ago. What would it feel like to run her hands through that thick hair of his?

Heat crept into her cheeks. Where the heck had that thought come from? Maybe Cheyenne was right —she did need to get out more. It had been several months since she'd gone on a date. That had to be the only reason her body kept having these visceral reactions to Knox. "Did you just take a nap?" she asked, not bothering to hide the surprise from her tone. She hadn't pegged him as the napping type.

"Yeah, I didn't sleep well last night."

A smile tugged at her lips. "Did you have a nightma—"

"I hate to tell you this," he interrupted, "but I heard mice in your attic. I could hear little claws scurrying across the ceiling. The cats might not be doing as good a job as you thought."

Cheyenne put both hands on her cheeks. "Oh no. I'll call pest control right away."

"No, don't do that," Lainey said. "We have traps somewhere in one of the closets. I'll find them and put them in the attic."

Knox crossed his arms. "Mice carry diseases. Don't you want a professional to handle it?"

She shook her head. "Not when I can fix the problem myself." She finished the last of her lunch and set the bowl in the sink. Then she poured a cup of coffee, adding cream and sugar.

"You're not afraid of much, are you?" he asked.

"Nope. Growing up on a ranch will do that to a person."

Cheyenne's phone rang. She pulled it out of her apron and glanced at the caller, then silenced it quickly. Just like she'd done at the parade.

"You don't have to ignore Damian's calls on my account. I'm headed back outside."

"I'm not doing it because of you," Cheyenne mumbled. "I'm not in the mood to talk to him right now."

"Oh." A spark of hope ignited in Lainey's chest. Had Cheyenne come to her senses and realized Damian wasn't right for her?

Cheyenne untied the apron, hung it on the hook, and walked out of the room with her shoulders lowered.

Something was bothering her sister. It made sense that Cheyenne didn't want to talk about Damian with Lainey, but Cheyenne also didn't talk about her singing career. What was going on? Would she ever open up to Lainey like she once had?

A low but distinct squeal came from the barn.

Lainey's heart skipped a beat. "Nutmeg."

She sped through the kitchen and mudroom without bothering to put on a coat. A mare typically labored heavily for only twelve to eighteen minutes. She had to hurry.

Outside, she ran to the barn, vaguely aware of Knox following behind her.

In the barn, Nutmeg lay on her side with her legs extended.

Lainey swallowed hard. She would do everything in her power to help Nutmeg and her foal. "Knox, I need you to get me a clean wrap for Nutmeg's tail, a towel, and latex gloves. Everything's in the supply room."

"You got it." He rushed to the back of the barn.

She filled a bucket with soap and water and stepped inside the stall.

"Hey, girl. We get to meet your baby today." Her voice was soft and soothing. Normally, she let mares labor on their own without any interference. But because Nutmeg's pregnancy was preterm, Lainey wanted to take every precaution to keep the foal healthy.

Knox returned and handed Lainey the supplies.

Nutmeg lifted her head and glanced at her hindquarters. A moment later, the horse pushed herself up on all fours. Milk dripped from her udders. Grunting, she lay down again on the straw.

Kneeling, Lainey worked quickly, placing

Nutmeg's tail in the wrap. She washed the mare's hindquarters with mild soap and water, then moved out of the way, into a corner of the stall.

Nutmeg continued grunting as a stream of liquid gushed out onto the straw.

"Is that …" Knox let the question trail off.

"Amniotic fluid?" Lainey finished.

He nodded. Even in the dim light of the barn, his face looked ashen.

She sent him a reassuring smile. Watching a horse's labor wasn't easy on the stomach. She needed to keep him preoccupied before he threw up, or worse, fainted. "Can you keep track of the time for me? How long do you think we've been out here?"

He glanced at his watch. "About ten minutes."

"OK."

The horse rose, this time urinating while she stood, then heaved her body onto the floor with a heavy breath.

Minutes ticked by as they watched in silence. With every passing minute, Lainey's stomach knotted with anxious tension. Where were the foal's feet? Why weren't they coming out yet?

Knox gripped the top of the stall door. "What's wrong?"

"Labor isn't progressing. How much time has passed in total?"

"Thirty minutes."

She tugged on the latex gloves and knelt by Nutmeg's tail. Inserting her hands inside the cervix, she felt for the foal's legs. It didn't take long to find them. She wrapped her fingers tightly around the little bony legs and waited until Nutmeg had a contraction, then she pulled.

Behind her, it sounded like Knox gasped, but she couldn't be sure. If the foal's life hadn't been in danger, she would've smiled at his surprise. "Come on, Nutmeg. You can do it, girl."

The foal's front legs and head appeared.

Lainey's forearms ached from the strain. She paused for a moment, waiting for another contraction. When it came, Nutmeg gave a final push, and the rest of the foal tumbled onto the straw.

Lainey scooted back a foot. Was the foal alive? There was no movement inside the torn sac.

"Is the baby OK?" Knox asked quietly.

Lainey held her breath, unable to answer.

Slowly, a head distinctively lifted, and the legs extended. The white sac stretched and tore farther, showcasing a small black foal.

A lump formed in her throat. The foal survived the labor. She needed to call Will to have a thorough veterinary examination right away, but for a second, she reveled in the moment. She glanced up at Knox, her chest rising and falling. Witnessing a new life come into the world was one of the most precious experiences.

He stared wide-eyed at the foal. "I've never seen anything like it." He met her gaze and held it. "You were amazing."

She grinned. "I'm glad you were here."

Oddly enough, she meant it.

———

That night, Knox collapsed into bed. His thighs were still sore from horseback riding, and a dull headache crept across his forehead. He pulled the quilt over his body and turned onto his side.

In the distance, a chorus of wolves let out long sorrowful howls.

Knox shivered. There had to be many dangerous creatures living in the woods. That could be a risk for people staying at the resort. His team would have to address that issue to ensure guests' safety.

When the howls subsided, silence settled across the loft.

No little claws scurried across the ceiling.

Lainey had been in Nutmeg's stall most of the day, but she must have come in at some point to set up mousetraps.

She was a nicer person than he'd given her credit for.

And watching her deliver the foal had been incredible. She'd known exactly what to do, not only with Nutmeg but with him. She'd been assertive when she'd needed to be, telling him what supplies she needed.

Despite her focused attention on the laboring mare, Lainey had also noticed when Knox was about to pass out. Having him keep watch of the time was clever and beneficial for everyone involved.

The most impressive part, above all else, was her gentle assuredness with Nutmeg. She was a natural nurturer with animals.

Warmth spread across his chest. She would be a good mother one day.

He turned onto his other side and fluffed the pillow. Why was he thinking about Lainey being a mother? It didn't matter.

Correction—it shouldn't matter.

Soon enough, she would just be a distant memory, one of Paul McKinley's granddaughters who sold her land to Mt. Point Development.

He flipped over to his back. Who was he kidding? Lainey Evans was one of the most interesting women he'd ever met.

CHAPTER
Nine

"LAINEY, WAKE UP."

She shifted slightly. The floor beneath her was hard, coated with a layer of straw. She blinked against the bright rays of sunlight pouring through the cobwebbed windows of the barn. *Huh?* She jolted upright, her muscles aching in protest.

Knox came into view first. He stopped in front of Nutmeg's open stall door, wearing sweatpants and a sweatshirt. His hands cupped a steaming mug. "You slept out here all night?"

She combed a hand through her hair and wiped drool away from her mouth. How embarrassing for Knox to find her like this. "I couldn't leave Cocoa."

"Cocoa?"

"Since his mom is Nutmeg, I thought his name should be Cocoa."

"I like it." Knox extended the mug to her. "This is for you. It's coffee with cream and sugar. I noticed that's what you put in it yesterday."

Her lips parted. He'd noticed how she took her coffee? "That was … kind of you."

She rose from the floor, wiping straw off her jeans and shirt. She reached for the mug. Taking a sip, she glanced at the foal. The little animal looked like a skeleton, with clumps of black hair sticking out in several spots. His joints were swollen and disfigured.

Knox's Adam's apple bobbed up and down. "What did the vet say after examining them?"

She expelled a heavy breath. "Nutmeg is in great condition, considering how unhealthy she was when she first arrived. Cocoa, on the other hand, has neonatal septicemia, which is a bacterial infection in his blood stream. It could be deadly. We caught it early, though, so the vet prescribed antibiotics. But those need to work fast because he has sores in his mouth, making it hard for him to nurse."

"How horrible."

She nodded. It would be an uphill battle for Cocoa.

Knox cleared his throat. "Quinn wanted me to tell you that she'll take a turn watching mama and baby if you have other things you need to do today."

She shifted her weight from one foot to the other. "I had planned on checking fences yesterday and didn't get to it. But I don't know. What if Cocoa takes a turn for the worse while I'm gone?"

"Then Quinn will call you." He reached over and untangled a piece of straw from her hair.

Her pulse quickened. "Thanks."

"Of course," he said in a husky tone. "Wouldn't want you walking around like that all day."

Heat flushed beneath her cheeks.

"So? Will you let your sister help?"

Lainey gave a slow nod. "OK."

"Great, and I'll go with you to check the fences."

"You don't have to do that. I'm sure you have your own work to do." A smile tugged at her lips. "There has to be plenty of land you want to take away from other homeowners."

"I bring you coffee, and this is how you repay me, by mocking my job?" Knox crossed his arms, his tone light. "I'll work when we get back. Plus, you're tired. Don't you want another set of eyes checking the fences?"

He smiled that dazzling smile of his, melting her reservations. "Can you get ready quickly?" she asked.

"Of course."

"How long does it take you to get ready in the morning?"

"An hour and a half, give or take. I usually go for a short run, eat, take a long shower, and do my hair."

"Did you just say 'do my hair'?"

"Yes, I did. What's wrong with that? I have great hair, and one day, it'll start falling out or turn gray, so I might as well enjoy it while I have it."

She rolled her eyes. His comment was a little conceited, but it wasn't bad reasoning. Most men would kill for a head of hair like his. "Meet me by the shed in thirty minutes. I'll go get the UTV ready."

"Is that like a four-wheeler?"

"Some UTVs are similar to four-wheelers, but the one we own is a two-seater cab. It also has heat, which is nice in winter," she explained.

"Oh. Great."

"If you're late, I'm leaving without you."

In the house, she quickly took a shower, spoke with Quinn, and packed lunches in a backpack. Then, she made her way to the garage behind the house where their large equipment was stored. She grabbed helmets and parked the UTV outside on the paved path.

Knox jogged toward her, wearing jeans, new cowboy boots, and a new Carhartt winter coat. "How did I do?" As he spoke, his breath came out in steamy clouds. "Was I fast enough for you?"

"Close enough. I'm impressed that you bought some new clothes. Your coat is much more appropriate if you're going to be outside for long periods of time." She handed him a helmet and adjusted her own over a French braid. "We'll drive slowly around the perimeter. Keep an eye on the fence and look for any wooden posts that are down or places where the barbed wire is sagging." She could've used more technical terms, but then he wouldn't have a clue what she was talking about.

He gave her a mock salute. "Got it, captain."

"Please don't do that again." Even as she said it, a chuckle escaped from her lips. She opened the driver's side door, turned on the engine, and cranked up the heat. Once Knox was settled, she drove the vehicle to the north side of the property and followed the fence westbound.

Sunlight glistened off the fields of snow, creating a glittery blanket over the grass.

"Wow. This is really pretty," Knox said over the loud drone of the engine. "It's nothing like seeing snow in the city."

She nodded in agreement, pleased. His appreciation for the view was a good start. Would it be possible to show him how sacred this land was to her family, though? Especially in a short amount of time? He wouldn't wait forever for an answer.

For the next two hours, they rode past the grazing horses and cattle. She pointed out several places as she drove by—the small cemetery where two generations of family were buried, the field where Grandpa first taught her how to ride a horse, and the large willow tree she used to climb to race her sisters to the top.

So many memories had been made over the years, deeply rooted in the land and then resurrected by the people who retold the stories. If someone else besides her family owned the land, the memories would lay dormant, forever forgotten.

And yet, five hundred thousand dollars was a lot of money. Even if she split it with her sisters, it was much more than Grandpa had given her to start the business. It was enough to build a bigger barn with more stalls, to buy plenty of food and straw, and to pay for veterinary care if necessary.

Lainey shook the thought away like a nagging bee. She'd be able to start the business, but then she'd lose the ranch.

If she acquired it at all. Were her and her sisters even close to meeting Grandpa's standards of coming together as a family? Quinn was gone most days, training with her coach. And conversations with Cheyenne tended to get heated more often than not.

Maybe Knox wouldn't be the one taking away her home. Maybe they'd lose it all on their own. Somehow, they needed to step it up.

As her mind wandered, she kept her gaze locked on the fence, searching for any inadequacies. The north and west sides were in good shape. She checked her watch. "Do you want to stop for lunch?"

Knox gave her a thumbs-up.

She parked in a spot that faced the majestic mountains and took off her helmet. After he set his helmet on his lap, she handed him a turkey and cheese sandwich, strawberries, a bag of trail mix, and a bottle of water. "It's amazing to think that when my great-grandfather bought this land, there was nothing here."

"Besides the haunted shack in the woods."

"Well, besides that." She rested her elbow on the console. "What I meant was, he built this entire ranch with his own two hands. It gives me pride to think his blood, sweat, and tears were poured into the walls of my house."

"That *is* impressive." Knox opened the trail mix and popped a handful into his mouth. "But it doesn't look like anything has changed since then."

"Just because something is old, doesn't mean it should be updated," she said. "Not everything has to be brand new. I fix what *needs* to be repaired—the barn door, fences, and equipment."

"In other words, you're more of a 'if it's not broke, don't fix it' kind of girl." He smiled. "I'm more of a 'beauty from the ashes' kind of guy."

"I think you're romanticizing it a bit."

"How so?" he asked.

She took his question seriously, carefully considering her answer. "I think you're so used to remodeling places that you can't see the beauty right in front of you."

"I did today."

"You did, but I bet you don't very often, do you?"

He was quiet for a moment. "No, not usually. As a developer, that's not how my brain works."

She turned toward him. "Why did you become a developer?"

"I've always loved fixing things. I get that from my dad. He was a mechanic. When I was a kid, I spent a lot of time in his garage. He taught me how to repair cars, trucks, and motorcycles. He also loved collecting old cars and restoring them."

"Somehow, I can't picture you with oil on your hands or grease and grime on your face."

"I don't mind getting dirty. I loved spending weekends in my dad's garage. He worked a lot just to make ends meet, so that was how we spent our time together."

Her eyebrows rose. Maybe she'd been wrong about him. Now that he was opening up, he didn't seem like a pretty boy who only cared about himself. "Is he still a mechanic?"

Knox shook his head. "No. My mom started a travel blog, and it really took off, so they bought a motor home, and now they take trips all over the US."

"I can't imagine not having a permanent home."

"Me either, but they love it. How about you? Where are your parents?"

"My mom is on vacation in Florida. And my dad left fifteen years ago. One night, he packed up his things and was gone by morning. He didn't even leave a note. I haven't seen him since."

The sympathy in his eyes reflected the sorrow in her heart. "That must've been hard to go through. Wondering where your dad went or why he left."

"Yeah. My family's never been the same. We drifted apart in many ways, turning to our own interests. My mom threw herself into taking care of the ranch, Cheyenne joined a band, and Quinn started competing."

"What about you? What did you throw yourself into?"

"Horses. I wanted to learn everything I could. Grandpa let me shadow him by watching his methods. Eventually, he let me train horses on my own with his guidance."

Knox reached out and grabbed her hand, gently rubbing his thumb against her palm. "Thank you for telling me. It explains a lot about your family."

She glanced down at their hands. His touch felt … soothing. Like soaking in a warm bath after a long trail ride. And yet, his comment was disturbing. Had she told him *too* much about her family? Could he use it to his advantage somehow? She quickly slipped her hand out of his grasp. "We, uh, we should finish checking the fences."

"Right." Red blotches traveled up his neck. He picked up the remains of their lunch and stuffed it into a grocery bag to throw away later.

She tucked a strand of hair behind her ear. He seemed just as flustered as she was. If only she could see his face to judge his reaction. But by the time he looked at her, he'd already put on his helmet.

She drove across the last stretch of fields. Why had Knox felt compelled to touch her so tenderly? Was it because of what she'd said, or had it been more premeditated, a tactic to get her to like him?

This was harder than she'd imagined. She was normally a straight shooter. Someone people counted on to tell the truth, whether they liked it or not. And she expected the same from others. Second-guessing what she was saying or questioning someone else's motives was *so* not her.

"Look." Knox pointed to a spot in the fence where there was a giant hole, big enough for horses or cattle to get through.

She shut off the engine and stomped through the snow, peering closely at the fence. *Uh-oh.*

Knox followed and stood beside her. "How did that happen?"

She carefully touched the wire. Clean cuts had sliced through the fence on both sides of the hole.

Her eyebrows pinched together with concern. "This was made with wire cutters."

"Why would someone do that?"

"I don't know." The bigger question was how long had the hole been in the fence? Had any livestock wandered off?

Blood pounded in her ears. She pulled out her phone and took a picture of the hole and the spots where the barbed wire was cut. "I need to call Amos and tell him to fix this right away. Then I'll ask Travis to count the cattle. I'll go back and check on the horses." She was talking to herself more than Knox, but she was keenly aware of his presence and kept her tone even.

Her gaze darted to the woods beyond as if the perpetrator was still around, hiding in the thicket. Who had cut a hole in their fence? Was it a stupid teenage prank, or was someone purposely causing trouble?

———

That afternoon, Knox sat at a small wooden desk in the loft. He sent an email to his team and closed the files for the smoothie shop and bookstore. Both projects were coming along nicely. The plumbing and electrical work had recently been completed at the smoothie shop, and the exterior of the bookstore had a fresh coat of paint.

He leaned back in his chair. What a day of surprises. Not only the hole in the fence but his conversation with Lainey. She'd opened up to him today and shared intimate details about her dad's absence.

That could only mean one thing. She was starting to trust him. It was a huge step in the right direction. He should be focused on that fact. And yet, what stuck with him more was that she'd grown up without her dad. No wonder she'd been close with her grandpa. He was the only father figure she'd known.

Despite how hard that must've been, she didn't complain about her upbringing. In fact, it seemed to have made her stronger. She was an inspiring woman. Which was why he'd instinctively reached for her hand. And for a moment, he'd forgotten why he was there.

She must've felt uneasy because she'd pulled her hand away, leaving him to realize what he'd done. Not the smartest move. He had a job to do.

Voices rose outside. He pushed the desk chair back and walked to the small window that over-looked the front yard. Lainey, Cheyenne, and Quinn stood outside near the wraparound porch. Lainey's back was to him. She had to be the one talking because her hands moved in wide motions and both Cheyenne and Quinn were looking at her.

He should get back to working and let them have a private conversation, but the temptation was too great, an itch that needed to be scratched. He pushed the window open an inch, causing it to creak.

He held his breath and peeked out the window. Had they heard the sound?

It didn't seem likely. Cheyenne and Quinn were still looking at Lainey, who now pressed a palm against her forehead. "Ten cattle escaped. Amos and Travis are out searching for them."

"I can go out and look too," Quinn offered.

"That would be great," Lainey said. "I'll take a turn taking care of Cocoa and Nutmeg."

"Do you want me to search as well?" asked Cheyenne.

"No. There's too much to do. Are you up for mucking stalls?"

A look of horror crossed Cheyenne's face. "Sure," she said slowly.

Knox chuckled. The famous country singer probably hadn't come close to horse manure in years.

Lainey's request did give him an idea. She obviously needed more help. Tomorrow, he'd see what he could do to lighten her load.

She dropped her hands to her sides. "This is a

disaster. If the cattle ruin someone's property, we'll have another lawsuit on our hands."

"We need to figure out who cut the fence," Quinn said. "It couldn't have been a prank. Everyone in Cherry Creek understands the importance of livestock. So, it had to be someone who *wanted* the cattle to get out."

"I agree, but who would do that to us?" Lainey let the question linger and glanced up at the loft.

He ducked down quickly. Did she think *he'd* done it?

Sabotaging the ranch to get the women to sell was not how he conducted business. He expelled a frustrated breath. This was the last thing he needed—Lainey and her sisters questioning his actions when he'd just started to gain their trust.

He waited a few more seconds, then sat upright and glanced out the window.

Lainey was facing her sisters again. He could only see her angled profile.

"Could Evelyn be behind it?" Cheyenne asked.

Lainey shook her head. "Evelyn doesn't like me, but she wouldn't vandalize the ranch. If anyone found out, Sam would never be re-elected for mayor. And she loves the prestige of being the mayor's wife. She wouldn't risk it."

"That's true," Quinn agreed. "And she believes

she'll win the lawsuit, so she has no reason to target us."

Lainey put her hands on her hips. "How do you know that?"

"I overheard her telling a group of old ladies at the café. But don't worry, Georgia walked over and interrupted before Evelyn could get on her soapbox. Georgia managed to get them talking about Salvation Army donations instead."

Lainey smiled, but a frown quickly replaced it. "If I end up owing a significant amount to Evelyn for the lawsuit, I'll have to use the startup money Grandpa gave me for the horse training business."

She was planning to start a new business? This was exactly what he'd been hoping to find out. A solid reason to take the money he offered.

"Grandpa wouldn't want you to use the money he gave you," Quinn said.

"I don't want to either, but I might not have any other options. We'll take a significant loss if we can't find the cattle."

Knox frowned. She didn't think she had any other options? Why hadn't she mentioned Mt. Point Development?

Cheyenne toyed with the hem of her dress. "I could help. I'll call my bank and see what I can do."

Lainey's mouth hung open. "No way. I wouldn't ask you to do that."

"You didn't. Let me just make the call, and we'll go from there."

Lainey hesitated before a smile returned to her face. "I have an idea. Remember when Grandpa organized a fundraiser after Cherry's Five and Dime caught fire?"

Quinn nodded. "He taught a horse clinic at our ranch on how to be gentle with abused horses, and then the Sutherlands cleared out one of their barns for square dancing. It was really fun, and the town raised enough money to pay for the cost of damages that insurance didn't cover."

"What if we organize a similar event?" Lainey asked. "I could teach a horse clinic and show people what I can do. So they can see what value I'd bring to training their horses."

"I love it. And if you want to have square dancing, I could sing," Cheyenne said. "Would you want to host the event here?"

"That would be amazing if you would sing. I don't think we should host, though. Not when someone purposely damaged our property recently."

"What about the Beartooth Equestrian Center?" Quinn suggested. "It has the arena, which is a good space for the horse clinic, and it also has a large event space. A lot of people have wedding receptions there, so it has the perfect setup for music and dancing."

Lainey twisted her braid around her finger.

"Unfortunately, that place costs a lot of money to rent. I heard Scarlett talking about it when her parents planned their thirtieth wedding anniversary there."

"Leave the event planning to me." Cheyenne lifted her chin. "I'm sure they won't say no if I offer to perform at their center."

Lainey's smile grew wider. "Let's talk about this more tonight. In the meantime, if you see anything suspicious, let me know."

Her sisters nodded as they went their separate ways.

Knox tugged the window shut and sat down at the desk to work on other projects. But it was hard to concentrate after overhearing that conversation. None of the women had brought up his offer. Had they even talked about it?

In most cases, owners made a decision quickly. But the Evans sisters were still in mourning, and now they were dealing with sabotage.

The circumstances were very different.

And concerning. Who had freed the cattle? Could it be the same person who wanted the resort built? The motive was certainly there, but how could someone get on the property unnoticed? Though the property was large, it would still be risky since Lainey was outside most of the day, and so were the men who worked for her.

Hmm. The ranch hands. Amos and Travis could have easily cut holes in the fence without Lainey giving a second thought to their whereabouts. They were here almost every day and often in the fields alone. Did either of them have a reason to vandalize the ranch and free part of the herd?

An unsettling feeling pricked his gut. No matter who did it, if there was a strong motive, the culprit would strike again.

CHAPTER
Ten

LAINEY STEPPED inside Cherry's Five and Dime, inhaling the scents of smoked meat and cheese.

At the front of the general store, Scarlett leaned against the counter of the post office reading a copy of *People*. Packages and outgoing mail were piled up behind her.

Lainey grabbed a cart and strolled past the post office. "Busy time of year, huh?"

"What?" Scarlett tore her gaze away from the magazine and laid it on the counter. A headline in bold font read "Cheyenne Evans and Damian Hart Call Off Secret Engagement."

Lainey stared at the article.

"I'm so glad you came in today!" Scarlett's eyes lit with excitement. "I can't believe your sister was secretly engaged to Damian Hart. Well, I'm sure it wasn't a secret to you. You probably already knew that she'd broken up with him too." Scarlett stood up straighter. "Is he still her agent even though they aren't together anymore?"

A lump formed in Lainey's throat. So that was why Cheyenne didn't want to talk to her boyfriend.

Scratch that—her fiancé.

Her ex-fiancé.

Cheyenne had been engaged and hadn't said a word to Lainey or Quinn. How could her sister keep that kind of news from them? Sure, they weren't close, but an engagement was a big deal.

Scarlett tucked a strand of red hair behind her ear. "I'll just ask Cheyenne when she comes in."

"OK." What else could she say? Lainey didn't have any information to share, and even if she did, she wouldn't talk to Scarlett about it.

It hadn't always been that way. Growing up eight miles apart, they'd spent a lot of time together riding the school bus, going for trail rides, and having sleepovers. But after Lainey ended things with Will and went off to college, they hadn't stayed friends.

That was life. People grew apart. Sometimes, they left and never came back. Lainey had learned that firsthand when Dad suddenly decided he didn't want to have a family anymore, packed all his things, and left. Months later, he'd sent divorce papers to the house.

She turned the cart away from the post office and pulled out her shopping list. She had a to-do list a mile long and thinking about Cheyenne and Dad weren't on it.

"Wait," Scarlett called after her. "We're almost out of Christmas stamps, so if you want a book or a roll, you should buy them soon."

Christmas. So consumed with daily responsibilities and preventing Knox from buying their ranch, she'd barely thought about it. Christmas was only three weeks away.

"I'll get stamps on my way out," she said with her back still turned.

Her chest ached with longing. Grandpa had played a pivotal role in their holiday traditions. They always opened their presents on Christmas Eve, then they would sit around the fireplace while he played guitar and sang. She closed her eyes for a brief moment, imagining his deep velvety voice, as soothing as honey on a sore throat.

Suppressing the array of emotions bubbling in her chest, she pushed her cart toward the aisle with horse feed and supplies. Nutmeg needed more grain to help with lactation. The mare's milk supply was low because Cocoa was still having difficulty latching on. Everyone at Lost Canyon Ranch had been taking turns hand-milking the mare every few hours, then feeding the milk to Cocoa. The foal needed more than what his mama could currently provide, so they'd also been supplementing with fresh goat's milk.

She glanced down at her list. She wanted to buy a variety of essential oils. Grandpa had used oils on many of their horses in the past, so it was worth a try to put some on Cocoa's muscles and joints to see if they would help ease his pain.

Rebel needed sugar beets and oats for his bran mash. Soon enough, the Appaloosa would be back to his normal weight, and he wouldn't need the extra nutrients. In the three short days Knox had been at the ranch, Rebel had gained ten pounds. The plan was working.

She loaded her cart and turned down the next aisle to look for a new notebook and pens. One of her goals this week was to draft a business plan. Before she reached the items, she stopped midstep.

Knox was at the far end of the aisle, chatting with Evelyn and Will.

Even though Will had come to the ranch to examine Nutmeg and Cocoa, seeing him on a regular basis would take some getting used to. Over the years, his skinny frame had filled out nicely. A plaid shirt fit snugly over his broad shoulders and muscular arms. He had a square jaw and striking blue eyes. She had no doubt many women found him attractive. But despite his good looks, she would only ever see him as a friend.

She slowly walked in their direction, eyeing the group of three with skeptical curiosity. This little powwow wasn't good. What had the Sutherlands said to Knox? What had he said to the Sutherlands?

Evelyn turned her head toward Lainey, her hand flying to her neck brace. "Oh, hello, Lainey."

"Evelyn," she said through clenched teeth. Did the woman actually need that contraption, or was she wearing it to make people feel sorry for her?

Maybe it was a good thing Knox was talking to the Sutherlands. Otherwise, she'd be tempted to tell the mayor's wife how upset she was about the lawsuit. Which wouldn't help her case. Knowing Evelyn, the woman would bring it up in court and say she was being bullied.

Will tipped his hat in greeting. "Nice to see you, Lainey."

"You too." She folded the shopping list and placed it in her pocket.

Evelyn pursed her lips and glared at Lainey. "I hope you're ready to settle during our mediation in a couple of weeks. There's really no reason to take this *situation* any further."

Lainey ran her tongue along the front of her teeth. "That depends on what you ask for."

Evelyn made a *humph* noise.

Will cleared his throat. "Mom, we should get going."

Evelyn nodded at her son. She put her hand on Knox's elbow, her tone warm and affectionate. "I'm glad we ran into you, Knox. If you need anything, don't be a stranger."

"That's very kind of you. I appreciate it." Knox sent her a hesitant smile.

Will tipped the brim of his hat again, his gaze lingering on Lainey as the pair walked to the front of the store.

Seriously? They were on a first-name basis? Knox must have used his charm to win over Evelyn. That was no easy feat. What had he done to gain her affections? The question lingered on her tongue, and yet, there were more important matters to discuss. "What were you talking to the Sutherlands about?"

"Don't worry. I didn't tell them *all* your secrets." Knox smirked. "I get the sense that Will already knows some of yours anyway. Let me guess. Is he an ex?"

She folded her arms across her chest. "Yes. We dated our senior year of high school. Now, answer *my* question."

"I asked them about this building. I found it interesting that the store was built with a mix of antique wood and newer distressed wood. Not only on the walls but the floorboards too. Will said the store caught fire ten years ago and that both of your families hosted a fundraiser."

Was it a coincidence that he'd brought up the fundraiser after she'd just discussed it with her sisters yesterday, or had he overhead them? "We did. In fact, we're planning to host a similar event soon."

"For what?"

Once again, she'd put her foot in her mouth. If she told him about the horse training business, he'd try to convince her that his offer would help with the startup.

And yet, he'd find out soon enough anyway. Nothing could stay secret in Cherry Creek for long. "Before my grandpa passed away, we were planning to start a horse training business. The event will raise awareness for my business and show people that they can trust my training methods despite what Evelyn is saying."

A spark of awe ignited in his creamy brown eyes. "That's a great idea." He leaned in close and lowered his voice. "Inviting everyone from town would give you an opportunity to watch people. See if anyone's acting strange."

The low huskiness of his voice mixed with the scents of lemon and amber coming from his cologne made it hard to focus. She took a step back, putting space between them, and glanced down at his cart—filled with storage bins and wooden containers.

Talk about strange. Why was he stocking up on organization supplies?

"Can I help in any way?" he asked.

"You could pass out flyers in the next couple of days. The venue had a cancellation for this Friday, so we have to let everyone know as soon as possible." She shifted her weight from one foot to the other. "Why are you trying to help me?"

He shrugged. "I don't want the lawsuit to affect the way people view you as a horse trainer. I've already seen how amazing you are with Rebel, Nutmeg, and Cocoa."

She swallowed hard. That was really sweet. "But you still want my ranch."

"Yes, I do. And I've been upfront and honest about it. I wouldn't do anything behind your back to get it."

Her chest rose and fell. He made a good point. Guilt tugged at her insides. If only she could say the same for herself.

"Have you and your sisters discussed my offer at all?" he asked.

Lainey pulled her braid over her shoulder, running her fingers over the intertwined locks. "With so much going on, we haven't had time to talk about it."

"I see." Disappointment was evident in the hard set of his jaw.

She glanced down at the floor where the new and old floorboards connected. Her previous thoughts and recent feelings toward Knox clashed in a similar fashion.

But just because he was a better man than she'd imagined didn't mean she should feel bad for planning to keep the ranch.

It was her home. The land of her forefathers, and she wasn't selling it to anyone.

Not even the man who could make her stomach flip-flop and her heart speed up like crazy.

———

On Friday, Knox settled onto the stadium seats at the Beartooth Equestrian Center. The seats surrounded a large sand-filled arena with plenty of space. Thanks to Cheyenne, the manager of the center had eagerly agreed to let her rent their facility for free as long they could post pictures for marketing purposes.

The double doors to the arena opened as people arrived—Floyd Isaacson, the lawyer; Hank Guthrie, the sheriff; followed by Scarlett and Will; Amos and Travis; and many familiar faces of those whose names Knox hadn't learned.

For a last-minute event, the turnout was good. About fifty people, give or take.

Fifty suspects who might have cut the fence and killed four cows.

Amos had found six missing cattle grazing

five miles away from Lost Canyon Ranch. The other four were not so lucky. They were found dead on the shore of Piney Creek. Someone had poisoned the water in the same area where the cows had taken a drink. It couldn't be a coincidence.

Losing four cows would cost them ten to twelve thousand dollars.

Worse than that, Lainey and her sisters had lost their sense of security. They hadn't come out and said it, but ever since Amos discovered the cattle, Lainey had been biting her fingernails, Cheyenne jumped at the slightest noises, and Quinn kept peering out the windows.

He couldn't blame them. It was alarming to think someone had purposely damaged their property and killed their livestock.

He had to be on high alert tonight, watching for signs of odd behavior. It could be anyone.

Georgia waltzed into the arena in pink cowgirl boots and a red furry coat.

Anyone except for Georgia. No way could a woman who dressed like her have a deep dark motive to kill.

She sat down beside him and removed her matching red earmuffs. "Why in the world did they plan something like this in two days? They should've scheduled it months out."

He gave her a playful grin. "And yet, you were still able to make it."

"That's because I'm an old single woman with nothing better to do."

"You're not old. You can't be more than forty."

She fluffed the bottom of her short curly hair, clearly enjoying his flattery. "I'm actually sixty-two."

He feigned surprise.

Georgia scanned the crowd. "Where's Quinn?"

"She's at the ranch taking care of a mare and its foal."

Voices quieted as Lainey led a gray horse into the arena. She stopped near the audience, her cheeks becoming a dark shade of crimson. She noticeably swallowed before lifting the microphone.

Knox smiled. Her nervousness was endearing.

"Thank you for coming. For as long as I can remember, people have brought troubled horses to my grandpa because they couldn't figure out what to do. Over the years, he transformed horses from being afraid of water to loving it, he nursed malnourished horses back to health, and he even taught blind horses to be reliable on trails."

She took an unsteady breath into the microphone. "I could go on and on with examples. But what I'd like to point out is that I was right by his side, watching and learning. I love horses. I value them and respect them." She gave a quiet chuckle. "Honestly, I prefer them over people."

Several people from the audience laughed.

"With your help, I would like to open a new facility at Lost Canyon Ranch where I can train horses. I want to be someone you turn to when you're out of ideas."

"I understand that you might not trust me, in light of recent events, but today, I'd like to show you what I can do." She gently caressed the gray fur between the horse's eyes. "When you bring a horse home, one of the first tasks you need to accomplish is getting the animal to wear a saddle. Usually, they buck. It could be because of physical or emotional issues, so you need to rule out all physical reasons first."

"Is it true Tori Sutherland broke her arm when one of your horses jumped over a fence?" The question came from a woman wearing an expensive-looking pantsuit, more suitable for a polo match than a clinic and square dancing.

Lainey pulled her shoulders back and lifted her chin. "As we all know, even when we're careful, accidents can happen."

A thick burly man adjusted a large belt buckle hidden beneath his protruding belly. "I heard your horse was unresponsive to your commands *before* you let Tori ride."

Lainey pursed her lips. "What happened that day was a fluke."

Knox had the sudden urge to speak up for her. The horse clinic was supposed to showcase her abilities, not create a stomping ground for people to judge her.

Lainey pulled on the horse's halter, bringing the mare around in front of her. "I'd like you to meet Sassy. Travis Jacobs, my ranch hand, recently bought this beautiful mare at an auction. He's letting me borrow her for the clinic. This is the first time I'm making an attempt to saddle her."

Knox shifted on the bleachers. *Please let this go well for Lainey.*

"Instead of using a saddle first, I'll start with this rope." Lainey created a loop and placed the rope around the horse's midsection. She made a clucking noise, and Sassy trotted in a circle around her. "I'll change the pressure and pull the rope a little tighter around her flank." As soon as Lainey pulled the rope, the mare lifted her back legs and bucked. "I'll keep the pressure on until she stops bucking, then I'll loosen it."

Knox grinned. Lainey was getting in her groove, all accusations and criticism forgotten. There was no denying she had a way with horses.

After several minutes of moving the rope to different spots on Sassy's body, Lainey loosened the rope and took it off. "Since she's stopped bucking, I'll use a blanket now. You always want to start with a material that's soft and light." Once Sassy stood still, Lainey rubbed the blanket over the horse's back.

The moment the blanket made full contact, Sassy's ears pulled back, and she tried to step away.

Lainey removed the blanket and set it in front of the horse's muzzle. The animal leaned forward and sniffed it. Lainey slowly moved to Sassy's other side and rubbed the blanket on her back again. The horse shook her mane but stayed in place. Lainey pulled a peppermint out of her pocket. "Good girl."

Scarlett thrust her hand in the air.

"Yes?" Lainey asked.

"These extra steps are a lot of work, and in my opinion, a waste of time. I've watched trainers at Serenity Stables put saddles on right away."

"There are horses you *can* do that with, but for many of them, they need to know you won't hurt them. They need to trust you. Plus, this is a great opportunity for you and your horse to get to know each other. It's all about bonding, especially at the beginning of your relationship."

Scarlett scowled. "You're talking about a horse as if it could be your friend."

"Well, yeah. The better you and your horse get along, the more she'll trust you. Developing trust doesn't happen overnight. You have to work at it."

Lainey held out another peppermint. "Treats can be useful during training. But some horses will take advantage of treats and won't listen to commands unless you give them one. You don't want to develop a bad habit, so you need to use your own discretion with each horse."

She picked up a pad and saddle.

The animal shifted, kicking up dust with her front legs.

Lainey stood on Sassy's left side and positioned the pad a few inches in front of the horse's withers, at the base of her neck. Lainey waited for a moment, then swung the saddle up and over, gently placing it on Sassy's back.

The horse stood still and let Lainey tighten the cinches.

"Usually, I'll let horses wear a saddle for five to six hours and put them out in the pasture with it on. I'll do this again every day for the next two to five days, depending on how well they adjust to wearing it." Lainey ran her hands through Sassy's mane. "See this? Sassy is standing still and not fighting me anymore."

The crowd clapped.

A wide grin spread across Lainey's face.

Cheyenne rose from her seat and stood in front of the audience. "That's the end of our clinic. I hope you can take what you learned from Lainey and use it on your own horses. If you make your way through the back doors of the arena, you'll find the event venue. There's a donation box on a table when you first walk in the room. We have appetizers and drinks, and in an hour, we'll start the square dancing." She stopped speaking and stared at someone in the crowd. Her face lost all its color. She quickly turned and walked out a pair of side doors.

Georgia lowered her spectacles and looked at Knox. "What was that all about?"

"I'm not sure." Had she seen someone she wasn't expecting? Knox scanned the stadium seats. Most people were on their feet, starting to make their way to the back of the building.

A lone figure caught his attention. A man in jeans, a suit jacket, and a cowboy hat walked quickly in the opposite direction, toward the front of the building.

"I'll be right back, Georgia." Knox followed the man from a distance, maneuvering through the crowd.

The man started jogging and slipped through the front doors.

Knox ran through the entryway. As he stepped outside, brisk air stung his face and seeped through his sweater. In his haste, he hadn't bothered to grab his coat.

Ignoring the cold, he walked farther into the

parking lot. The guy had to be out here somewhere. But there was no sign of him. Just parked cars.

The quiet chill sent shivers down Knox's spine. Who was that man? And why had he rushed away?

Knox squeezed the back of his neck. This was ridiculous. He was paranoid. The man could've received a phone call and had to leave unexpectedly. With so many ranchers and farmers in Cherry Creek, there were numerous possibilities and emergencies. Or maybe the man hadn't wanted to stay for square dancing.

But then why had he run away?

Knox took one last look at the parking lot and turned back toward the equestrian center. Whatever the case was, he would have to talk to Lainey and her sisters. He might not say anything tonight, though. There was no reason to ruin their evening. He, on the other hand, would stay vigilant.

———

After getting Sassy settled in the barn near the arena, Lainey went in search of Cheyenne. Inside the event room, Christmas lights highlighted the stage and dance floor, platters of food and drinks were spaced out along a bar that stretched across the back, and holiday centerpieces were placed on all the tables, tastefully made out of wooden planter boxes filled with candles, juniper, and pinecones.

Wow. In all the times she'd come to watch equestrian competitions, she'd only ever seen the arena and horse barn. This place was amazing. Friends had asked her to come here before, wanting to go out for a girls' night, but she'd always turned them down. A night out had consequences. She'd be up before dawn no matter how late she stayed out, and then she'd be more tired than she already was. It wasn't worth it.

But she'd enjoy tonight. As long as she could find her sister and make sure Cheyenne was all right. Her sister wasn't on stage, eating at one of the tables, or making small talk with townspeople. Where could she be?

There was only one other place Cheyenne would go.

The bathroom. If no one else was in there, maybe Lainey could finally broach the subject of Cheyenne's engagement. She'd been trying to bring it up for the last two days, but between the poisoned cattle and planning this event, it hadn't felt right. Neither was tonight, really, not before her sister would sing in front of a crowd, but she had to bring it up soon.

Sure enough, Lainey found her sister standing in front of the vanity, reapplying mascara.

Cheyenne had changed into a sparkly navy dress

with long dangling earrings and a matching gold necklace. She stood back and assessed her work before twisting the cap of the mascara back on. Beneath the makeup, her sky-blue eyes were bloodshot.

Had her sister been crying? Lainey chewed on her thumbnail.

"What happened in the arena?" she asked quietly.

Cheyenne set the tube of mascara in her small makeup bag and zipped the case closed. "What happened with the cattle has me on edge. It's making me crazy."

"Did you see something that scared you?"

Cheyenne fluffed her hair. "I thought I saw someone pulling out a gun. But he was just adjusting his pants."

Lainey leaned against the wall. "Most people in Cherry Creek carry guns on them."

"Yeah, I know. I mean, I should've known. Like I said, I'm on edge. That's all."

Lainey nodded. She couldn't disagree. But more than fear weighed on her. It was her protectiveness. The ranch was her responsibility. Nothing like this had ever happened when Grandpa was in charge.

Cheyenne tucked the makeup case inside her large purse. "We should get back to the party. People will wonder where we are."

"Can I ask you something first?"

"Sure."

"Why were you crying?"

Cheyenne noticeably swallowed. "I don't want to talk about it."

"Does it have something to do with Damian?" The question was out before she could stop it. So much for waiting for the right time.

Cheyenne stared at the floor.

"I know you broke up. I saw it in *People*. How come you didn't say anything? Or tell me that you were engaged?"

"I didn't think you'd care."

Her sister's response struck a nerve. It was the same thing Lainey had assumed for the way Cheyenne left all those years ago. "Being engaged is a serious life decision. It must've been hard to break it off. Are you OK?"

Cheyenne transferred her purse from one hand to the other. "Yes. Well, I will be. I caught him cheating on me the day I was supposed to fly out for Thanksgiving. That's why I cancelled my flight." She took a breath before she continued. "I wasn't ready to end it right away, especially since he was also my agent. But after spending some time back here on the ranch, I finally got the clarity I needed. I called him, ended the engagement, and fired him as my agent."

"How awful."

"That's it? No 'I told you so'?"

"Nope. It doesn't matter now. Your well-being and happiness are what matter most."

Her gaze locked with Cheyenne's, relief and shock radiating through her core. She'd finally had an honest conversation with her sister without arguing.

Cheyenne sent her a shaky smile. "I appreciate you saying that."

"I'm here for you," Lainey said.

"Thanks."

When they returned to the room, the party was in full swing. "Ring of Fire" played from the speakers. Many people sat around tables, talking and laughing, some stood in line for drinks, and a handful of older couples were already out on the dance floor.

Knox stood by the bar with a group of five women. He wore jeans and a stylish gray sweater that made him appear much more sophisticated than many of the other men wearing plaid shirts. As he spoke, the ladies couldn't keep their eyes off him. He certainly had a way of charming the women in this town.

Somehow, she'd become one of them. Heat traveled up her neck. She lifted long blond locks off her clammy skin and tore her gaze away. No way would she be caught looking.

She swayed to the rhythm and mouthed the words—she didn't dare sing aloud because her voice sounded like sandpaper. Very different from Cheyenne's rich contralto or Grandpa's velvety bass.

Cheyenne tapped the microphone. "How's everyone doing tonight?"

Hoots and hollers sounded across the room.

"That's what I like to hear." Cheyenne thrust a fist in the air. "Let's start off the night right. I want everyone to dance to this one."

She took a quick breath, then started "Sweet Montana Home."

Many people rose from their seats. Knox held his hand out to Georgia and led her onto the dance floor. They linked hands and swung them up and down. The older woman laughed at something he said, a light sparking in her eyes that hadn't been there in a long time.

Lainey grinned. Georgia didn't let loose often. Her life revolved around the Wagon Wheel Café, keeping tabs on everyone, and not much else. People said that Georgia had been engaged once, but she'd stood him up at the wedding. When she didn't show, the groom-to-be moved out of town. She hadn't dated anyone since. No doubt she was lonely.

Floyd Isaacson sauntered over; his quirky smile contagious. He took off his hat and bowed. "May I have this dance, Miss Lainey?"

"Of course, Floyd."

His long, thin hand captured hers as he led her

onto the dance floor. "So, you, Cheyenne, and Quinn planned this event?"

"Yes."

"Good." He twirled her around clumsily. "And how are you getting along at home?"

She frowned. "We've had our share of arguments. It's hard living under one roof when Cheyenne has been gone for so long. We can't seem to agree on much."

His feet stopped moving for a second. "Don't forget what Paul expressed in his letter. If the three of you can't work together, then you won't get the ranch."

She quickly eyed Knox, who was dancing on the other side of the room. Thankfully, he couldn't have overheard what Floyd said. If he knew she didn't actually own the land yet, he would be furious.

The song ended, and Floyd squeezed her hand. "I'm rooting for you."

"Thanks."

She left the dance floor and walked to the bar to order a beer. That conversation had left her depleted. Planning this event together wasn't proof enough for Floyd to give them the ranch. He wanted to hear that they were getting along. That the everyday dealings at the ranch were a team effort.

On the dance floor, Knox gave Georgia a hug and

sauntered across the room to Lainey. "You're thinking about the ranch, aren't you?"

She folded her arms across her chest. "Why would you say that?"

"Because you had this terribly serious expression on your face." He leaned forward, his lips lightly brushing against her ear. "Don't worry, I might look like I'm having fun, but really, I'm watching everyone closely."

She shivered from his breath on her skin and swallowed hard. "I appreciate it. You can have a little fun, if you want."

"See, the thing is, I can't have fun unless you are."

"Is that so?"

"It sure is." He smirked. "And I'm not sure you know how."

She gave him a playful shove. "That's not true."

"Oh, yeah? Prove it."

On stage, Cheyenne started singing "Let Your Love Flow."

Knox turned toward Lainey and held out his hand, palm up. "Prove it by dancing with me. That's the only way I'll know for sure."

She should say no. But the word wouldn't come out.

The dimple appeared in his chin as he gave her that charming smile of his. "I promise I'll be a better dance partner than the lawyer."

He'd noticed her dancing with Floyd? "Fine." She kept her tone flat and rolled her eyes, hiding the pleasure buzzing through her veins.

Wasting no time, Knox swept her onto the dance floor in one fluid movement. He wrapped his arm around her waist, placing his hand on the small of her back and moving to the rhythm of the song.

The beat sped up, and he lifted his arm, twirling her in a circle. When she faced him again, he pulled her closer. Only an inch remained between them. "See, this isn't so bad."

She looked up into his eyes, reminding herself to breathe. But it was. It was very, very bad. Because this wasn't going to end well. She already knew the outcome. She wouldn't sell the land, and then he'd be angry with her. He'd go back to Seattle and never speak to her again.

Her chest constricted. Somehow, she'd have to live with the consequences.

CHAPTER
Eleven

KNOX HIKED behind Lainey up a steep, narrow trail, scanning the woods for Rebel. After getting home late last night, Lainey had gone into the barn to check on the horses. She'd found Quinn asleep in Cocoa and Nutmeg's stall and Rebel missing from his. This time, the horse couldn't have freed himself. Not with a new dead bolt lock on his stall door.

Someone had unlocked it on purpose.

Unfortunately, that wasn't the only act of sabotage last night. The donation box had gone missing before Lainey had a chance to count the amount and find out how much she'd raised.

His protective instincts had kicked into high gear. He wouldn't let anything bad happen to Lainey or her sisters.

Except for when he took away their land.

The thought emerged like an unwelcome visitor on Christmas morning.

No, he refused to look at it that way. He was providing an opportunity for them to start a new chapter in their lives.

Pushing the thoughts away, Knox scanned the woods for Rebel. They'd already searched the homestead, so they'd decided to split up and search farther. Cheyenne and Quinn rode on horseback by the creek, Amos had taken the UTV to explore the lowlands, while Knox and Lainey hiked up the mountainside.

He stopped and put his hands on his hips. His lungs burned. Apparently, all those hours of running on a treadmill at the gym hadn't prepared him for hiking in the mountains.

Not that he noticed the burn too much. The view in front of him was pleasantly distracting. Every step caused Lainey's jeans to squeeze tighter around her thighs. Her hips twisted from side to side, accenting her firm backside. Last night while they'd danced, it had taken all his restraint not to move his hands from those hips, to let them roam over her back and pull her against him.

"Do you see any signs of Rebel?" Lainey asked. Her voice held an edge of hysteria.

Knox put his hand on her shoulder and squeezed.

"Don't worry. We'll find him." His response came out breathy.

She must have noticed because she picked up a thick stick about hip height. After examining it, she handed it to him. "Here, use this. It'll help you get up the steep part, then the path will even out a bit."

"Thanks." He dug the stick into the ground as he climbed forward. She was right. It did help.

He pushed forward, refocusing. They had to figure out who had let Rebel escape. The culprit must have shown up while everyone else was at the concert, found Quinn asleep, and quietly unlatched Rebel's stall. "I have something I should tell you."

Lainey stopped and turned to look at him. "What is it?"

"As soon as the horse clinic was over, there was a man who jogged out of the arena, almost like he didn't want anyone to notice him. I thought it was strange, so I followed him, but when I got outside, I didn't see a soul. I think he was hiding from me."

She scrunched her nose, looking way too cute for him to completely focus on their conversation. "Why didn't you tell me this sooner?"

"I didn't have the heart to ruin your evening. And at the time, I figured he could have had many reasons for leaving early."

"But you don't anymore."

"No. I think the man who left came straight to the ranch to let Rebel escape."

She continued hiking, scanning the woods around them. "But how could he have taken the donation box, then?"

Good point. "What if it's not just one person? What if there's two of them?"

She rubbed her temples. "I have been concerned that it could be one of my men. It's possible Amos and Travis are working together. I still don't see why they'd do that to us, though. We're the reason they have paychecks."

"What about your ex?"

"Will? No way. He doesn't have a vicious bone in his body."

"Look," Knox whispered. He pointed to a thicker part of the woods where the sun slipped through the foliage.

A deer and its fawn strode through the long grass. The mom's ears perked before she nudged the baby with her nose, as if to say, *Be careful. Let's go.* Seconds later, they frolicked away.

"Do you see a lot of wildlife along this trail?" he asked. Not only was he curious, but he also wanted to distract her, to prevent her from worrying about the sabotage, if only for a moment.

"Oh yeah. We've seen foxes, beavers, coyotes, wolves, bears … just to name a few."

Hmm. Rails would need to be built along the private trails traveling from the dude ranch resort. Guests would love seeing the wild animals in their natural habitat.

Lainey glanced at him for a second, then continued climbing.

Did she sense he was lost in his own thoughts, planning how to make changes instead of seeing the beauty in front of him?

Maybe she was right—it might be a bad habit, after all. At least his question had distracted her.

They hiked in comfortable silence for half a mile before a flat clearing became visible ahead. He bent over, resting his hands on his knees. When he got back to Seattle, he'd have to find a new workout regime. Obviously, his current one wasn't cutting it.

The thought of going back to Seattle pricked his chest unexpectedly. Once this deal went through, he'd have no reason to see Lainey again.

Her phone broke the silence, playing "Let It Snow." She quickly pulled it out of her coat pocket and accepted the call. "Hey, Quinn." She paused to listen, then let out a low growl. "Hold on. You're cutting out." She moved a few inches to the left. "What did you say?" She paused to listen again. "Does he look hurt?" She clutched a hand to her chest. "Thank God. I'm so relieved."

She glanced at Knox and smiled. "My sisters

found Rebel grazing near the highway. This situation could've ended very badly if he'd crossed the road."

"It could have, but it didn't. Rebel's one smart horse. You've said so yourself." He returned her smile, equally relieved. Over the last two weeks, Knox had grown quite fond of the horse.

He straightened and took in their surroundings. A small mountain chickadee flew overhead, landing on a rock protruding over a crystal-clear reservoir. The opposite side of the lake was bordered with a red wall of dirt. Mountains loomed above the wall with a vast blue sky behind them. "This is breathtaking."

"It's one of my favorite places. It's so quiet and peaceful."

"Can we stay here for a little while? I'm sure you're itching to go back and check on Rebel, but Quinn did say he's all right, and this view is hard to walk away from."

Lainey chewed on the inside of her cheek. "Just for a bit." She stepped closer to the lake. "Want to dip your toes in?"

"Uh, isn't it freezing?"

"Yup." She pulled off her boots and two thick pairs of socks.

He stood still. "Why would we do that?"

"Why not?" She grinned. "Stop being such a baby."

He followed Lainey to a spot where a long, flat

rock jutted out over the lake. He settled down next to her, his shoulder brushing against hers as he threw off his own boots and socks, then rolled up his jeans.

She slipped her feet in the water and nudged his ribs with her elbow. "Go on."

"You're crazy."

"You're stalling."

Knox dipped his toes in the ice-cold water. The bitter temperature took his breath away. He immediately yanked his feet out.

She laughed and kicked water up at him.

"Hey, that was uncalled for." He chuckled, stuck his hand in the reservoir and splashed her back.

Lainey tried to lean away, but water splattered against her cheek. "You better watch it, or I'll push you in."

He shuddered. "No, don't do that. I give up. You started it, though."

"Oh, sure. Blame it on me." Laughing, she took off her hat and lay down with her back on the rock. She closed her eyes. The sun gleamed down on her head, making her naturally blond highlights appear lighter.

Without contemplating it, he lay next to her and closed his eyes.

"This was a good idea," she said quietly. "According to Cheyenne, I don't take enough breaks. She's probably right."

He opened his eyes and turned onto his side, propping up on one elbow. "I don't either. Usually, they make me feel antsy, like I should be getting something done."

"What do you do for fun in Seattle?" she asked.

"I work."

"No, seriously. What do you do for fun, outside of work?"

"Sometimes, I go to concerts with my buddies or stay at home and read a novel or go to Pike Place Market. If I'm downtown, I'll walk by the gum wall and stick some gum on it."

She turned onto her side as well and looked at him. "Huh?"

He chuckled. "There's a wall downtown where everyone sticks their chewed gum. It's a staple in Seattle."

"That's not weird at all." Her voice was laced with sarcasm. "It explains a lot about you, though."

"I'm sure it does." He grinned. "In all seriousness, I don't hang out with my buddies as much as I used to. Most of them are recently married. Which is why I spend my free time working instead."

"And here you were, giving me crap for not having fun when it sounds like you don't either." She shook her head, her expression morphing from playful to contemplative. "Have you ever been close to getting married?"

"No. Not even close."

"Don't tell me you're one of those guys who wants to stay single forever."

"No, actually, I can't wait to get married and start a family." He hesitated to say more, but the way she was looking at him—with such keen interest—kept him going. "I'm hoping to become vice president of Mt. Point Development soon. Once I get the position, I won't have to travel as often, and I'll actually have time to devote to a family."

"Do you think you'll get it?"

"Possibly. It depends." He wasn't trying to be elusive, but if he told her the truth, she might think he was purposely putting pressure on her.

A slight wind picked up, blowing loose strands of hair across her face.

He tucked the strands behind her ear. It would only take one swift motion for him to lean in and kiss her.

What would her reaction be? He licked his lips. So tempting.

A lump, the size of a large rock, formed in his throat. What was he thinking? It didn't matter what her reaction would be because it wasn't a good idea. Kissing her would complicate things even more.

She noticeably swallowed, the electric tension between them palpable. "What does the promotion depend on?"

He sighed. She wouldn't let this go. "If I can get the land for the dude ranch resort."

"Oh." Lainey sat up, rolled her jeans down to her ankles, and slid both pairs of socks over her feet. "We should get back. I need to check on Rebel."

"Are you upset?"

"No. Why would I be upset?"

Because you sound upset. Not that he would tell her that. Instead, he sat up and put his hand beneath her chin, willing her to look at him. "I didn't want to tell you about the promotion. As much as I'd like you to sell the land, I want you to do it for you."

"Is that the truth? That's really how you feel?"

"Of course. I've always believed it's a good deal."

Lainey's lips parted. Her chest rose and fell.

He blinked several times, reminding himself why he was here. It wasn't to fall for a cowgirl in Montana.

———

"I'm glad you're having a good time, Mom." In the mudroom, Lainey zipped her coat and slipped on a warm winter cap beneath her cowgirl hat before heading outside to the barn. "What are you up to today?"

"I'm at the beach."

"It's hard to imagine you sitting still on a beach towel."

"Well, believe it. I even have a tan."

"I'm jealous." Shivering, Lainey walked outside toward the barn to work on the ranch's finances, start her business plan, and give Cocoa his medications. The antibiotics were doing their job, and the sores in his mouth were smaller and seemingly less painful because the little foal was finally nursing. The essential oils were also helping. He was slowly getting better. But he still wasn't in the clear yet. Only time would tell.

She opened the doors to the barn, and her jaw dropped. "Uh, Mom, I have to go."

"What's wrong?"

"Nothing. I'll call you later. Love you." Lainey slipped her phone into her coat pocket, taking in the sight. Someone had reorganized the barn. All the tools that had been sitting out were placed in storage bins. The rakes and shovels hung from newly installed wall mounts. The wheelbarrow was pushed off to the side, and the floor had been swept.

She smiled. Knox bought the storage supplies at Cherry's Five and Dime because he'd planned to clean the barn.

But why? Was he trying to prove her wrong by acting like the good guy? Acting like he wanted to get to know her? To kiss her?

Her stomach fluttered at the memory. The desire in his eyes when he'd glanced at her lips this morning … *Whoa.* That couldn't have been an act, could it?

If it wasn't an act, then he had feelings for her.

Which wasn't good either.

He wanted a promotion. And he wouldn't get one because of her. Guilt formed a tight knot in her stomach. If only there was a way for both of them to get what they wanted. But they were on opposite ends of the tug of war rope, and only one side could win.

She expelled a deep breath. Time to get to work. To keep busy. That was the best way to deal with unwarranted thoughts.

The horses whinnied as she walked to the back of the barn and stepped inside Grandpa's office.

No way. Knox had reorganized this room too. She cupped a hand over her wide-open mouth. Grandpa's worn wooden desk wasn't cluttered anymore. Pens, pencils, highlighters, and a random assortment of office supplies had been placed inside a plastic desk organizer. Loose papers were in a tidy pile labeled with sticky notes. Grandpa's dinosaur of a computer sat in the middle of the desk. The black screen was clean, free from the smudges and dust that had been there yesterday.

She willed her feet to move farther into the room, her gaze traveling to the walls. They looked different. She peered closely at the faded paint and ran her pointer finger across the wall. Not a speck of dirt clung to her finger. *Holy cow.*

Her eyes glistened. This was one of the nicest things anyone had ever done for her.

And yet, she had to wonder about his motives. Was Knox stepping up his game to acquire the ranch and earn the promotion? Or was he making the best of his time while he was waiting for her decision?

Lainey sank into Grandpa's leather chair and looked out the window. The sky was gray and light snowflakes spiraled through the air. Those flakes were just the beginning. A storm was coming. Maybe the weather would keep the saboteur away. Then she could focus on what really mattered. Like planning for spring, how to make up for the loss of the cattle, and drafting a business plan.

She opened a drawer and took out the record books. She needed to go over all the numbers—the precise number of cattle, their weights, and pasture rotations. After that, she'd check the cash flow being spent on the horses—food, veterinary bills, and stall bedding.

She rested her elbows on the desk and rubbed her temples. It would be so much easier to give in to Knox. Take the money. Use it to pay off court expenses, purchase more cattle, and buy the equipment necessary for horse training.

But the easy route meant giving up. Grandpa

wouldn't want them to sell. He believed in her. She had to do everything in her power to make his dreams—her dreams—come to fruition on their family ranch.

Heavy footsteps approached the open door. Amos ambled inside, his ample belly almost covering his large belt buckle. Bags hung under his eyes. "Evening."

"I wasn't expecting to see you at this hour. What are you still doing here?"

He struck a match, holding the lit tip to his cigarette. He took a slow drag. "A storm is brewin'. I wanted to make sure the cattle were fed extra to get them through the next few days."

"Thank you."

He glanced at the office, his bushy eyebrows pinching together to form a momentary unibrow. "What the hell happened to this place? Did you clean?"

She chuckled. "No, Knox did."

He blew out a puff of smoke. "I've been wanting to talk to you about him. You should tell him to leave."

"Leave? Why?"

"Ever since he arrived, we've had trouble."

"The timing does line up, but whoever's messing with us is someone who understands ranching, which definitely isn't Knox."

Amos smashed the tip of his cigarette in the ashtray on Grandpa's desk. "You ain't thinkin' it's me, are you?"

She pushed back her shoulders. He wouldn't like her answer, but she had to be straight with him. "I'm looking at everyone as a possibility."

Amos grunted. "Everyone except the developer who has the most obvious motive." He ran a wrinkled hand down his thick beard. "I've worked for Paul for over two decades. He trusted me. And you've known me your entire life. I can't believe you're considering *me*."

"That's not what I said. I'm not ruling people out. I want to be smart about this."

He moved closer and leaned over the desk, pointing a stubby finger at her. "I've seen the way you've been lookin' at that city boy. You think it's smart to fall in love with him? He'll eat you up and spit you out, darlin'. He doesn't care a lick about you or this ranch."

Heat flushed up the back of her neck. Fall in love? That wasn't what she was doing at all. She was spending time with Knox, showing him how important this ranch was so he'd give up when she finally told him she wouldn't sell.

But the argument fell dead on her lips. Because she couldn't deny her feelings any longer.

———

The scent of potato soap, homemade bread, and cherry pie floated up to the loft. Knox's mouth watered. Dinner must be ready.

He descended the stairs, anticipation thrumming through his veins. What had Lainey thought when she'd walked into the barn? When she'd seen the office? Hopefully, he hadn't offended her, and she'd understood he was trying to make things easier for her. She deserved it.

His cell phone vibrated on the desk in the loft. He turned around and went back upstairs.

Boss Man.

With Montana being one hour ahead of Washington, Vince was still at the office.

Before Knox answered, he shut the door. He couldn't take the chance of anyone overhearing him. "Hi, Vince."

"Tell me the granddaughters have accepted the offer."

"Not yet." Knox sank down on the bed. He could only imagine the look of disappointment on his boss's face.

"I'd hoped to have the contract signed by now. You need to be more aggressive."

In all the years he'd worked at Mt. Point Development, Vince had never used the word *aggressive*. "Is there something I'm not aware of?"

Silence settled over the line.

"I'd rather you be frank with me," Knox said.

His boss blew a long exhale into the receiver. "The client isn't happy with you. G. S. thinks you're goofing off and focusing too much of your attention on Lainey Evans." Vince paused before continuing, "Is that true?"

His chest tightened. Even though the door was closed, he lowered his voice to a whisper. "Lainey is one of Paul McKinley's granddaughters. Of course, I'm focusing on her. I need her to trust me. Otherwise, this project will never happen."

"That's what I told the client. I said you're not the kind of guy to get mixed up with a woman, especially at the risk of losing a property."

At least his boss had faith in him.

And yet, the client's fear wasn't completely misplaced. Lainey was unlike any woman he'd ever met. Despite the long hours and hard work, she found joy in taking care of her ranch and her horses. She made him feel comfortable opening up and sharing about his life. It felt like he'd known her for much longer than two weeks.

"I have no reason to be concerned, do I?" Vince asked.

Knox rose and paced back and forth across the

loft. Lainey *was* a concern. So was the saboteur. But he didn't want his boss to worry.

"No, sir." He stopped pacing. How could he redirect this conversation? "Is there any way the client would change their mind about divulging their identity? If I knew who it was, we could collaborate, and I could get their advice on how to get the grand-daughters to sell."

"I'll touch base with G. S. and get back to you. Keep in mind, Knox, Christmas is two weeks away. I need to see more from you."

"Got it." He tossed the phone on his bed and raked a hand through his hair. Would Lainey and her sisters have an answer before then?

CHAPTER
Twelve

LAINEY PLOPPED down on the faded leather sofa across from the stone fireplace and draped a blanket over her legs. Two large windows flanked both sides of the fireplace, revealing thick snowflakes spiraling through the air. Despite the dropping temperatures outside, the room was filled with warmth.

Knox sat down on the opposite end of the couch, and Cheyenne nestled into Grandpa's recliner. Quinn was in her room, replaying clips of her competitors' races.

Outside, the wind howled in the darkness, causing the house to creak.

Lainey reached for her glass of wine. Maximus curled up on the floor nearby, resting his head above her feet. She took a sip of wine, eyeing Knox over the rim of her glass. "Thank you again for cleaning the barn and the office."

"I was happy to do it." Knox smiled, but it didn't quite reach his eyes.

She frowned. Ever since last night, he'd been off. He'd come down for dinner, his shoulders tight and his jaw clenched. He hadn't relaxed since.

He pointed at one of the pictures on top of the mantle. "Is that you and Quinn in karate uniforms?"

Lainey nodded. "Cheyenne did it, too, for a little while."

Her sister scoffed. "A few months at most. I kept breaking my nails. Lainey and Quinn were in it for ten years. They're both black belts."

Knox pretended to shudder and shifted away from her. "Yikes. Remind me not to make either of you mad."

"You better remember that yourself." She wiggled her fingers. "You're looking at lethal weapons." She punched him playfully in the arm, her knuckle hitting rock hard biceps. *Wow.* For a city guy, he stayed in good shape.

Cheyenne coughed and lightly hit her chest.

"Are you all right?" Lainey asked.

Cheyenne nodded, still coughing. "Wrong pipe," she managed to get out. But she wasn't looking at Lainey; she was staring at her phone. "I, uh, I'll be right back." She stood and walked out of the living room, disappearing from view as she strode down the narrow hallway.

Knox took a swig of beer. "You think it's her agent?"

"She doesn't have one anymore. She fired him."

"Oh."

"It's for the best. After Christmas, I'm sure she'll head back to Nashville and find a better agent." Lainey frowned. The thought of her sister leaving didn't appeal to her like it once had. But Cheyenne had a life elsewhere, a career that thrived in Nashville, so there wasn't any reason for her to stay.

When her sister left, what would life look like in Cherry Creek? Would they own the ranch for good, or would Floyd decide they hadn't measured up? In either of those scenarios, Knox would be gone as well.

She took another sip of wine and set down her glass, unwilling to consider how she'd feel when the time came.

Knox turned to face her, resting an arm on the back of the sofa, his hand close to her shoulder. "I've thought about what you said a few weeks ago—about only seeing what needs to be fixed—and I think you're right. I'm constantly in my head, and I'm missing what's right in front of me."

Her breath caught in her throat. The way he looked at her—all intense and serious—made her wonder if he was alluding to something else. Like, did he think he was missing out on her?

No, probably not. She was reading too much into his statement. But he'd thought about what she said. Now *that* was sweet. "It's not necessarily a bad thing. It makes you good at your job. But on a personal level, it's kind of sad. You aren't seeing the value in your surroundings."

He was quiet for a moment. "Live and learn, right? It's not too late to change. I have a lot of life left to go."

"How old are you?" she asked.

"Twenty-eight. What about you?"

"Twenty-six."

"Huh."

She crossed her arms. "What's 'huh' supposed to mean?"

He gave a nervous chuckle. "I would've guessed a little older."

"Wow, thanks a lot. You realize that could be offensive, right?"

"Sorry. I didn't mean it that way."

"Oh yeah? Then what did you mean?" She kept her tone lighthearted. His comment hadn't actually offended her, but it was fun to pretend.

"You have a quiet sort of confidence that makes you seem wiser than a twenty-six-year-old."

She smiled. "I guess I can't be mad at you, then."

"That's good. I wouldn't want you to karate chop me." He set his beer on the end table and raised his fisted hands in mock defense.

The flirtatious banter caused excitement to bubble in her chest. "You're not out of the woods just yet. You better be nice." She tried to lightly punch him in the chest.

He grabbed her wrist before she could make contact and pulled her close. His eyes filled with surprise—he clearly hadn't intended on bringing her this close to his face, but when she didn't pull away, his surprise morphed into desire. His gaze flickered to her lips.

Breathe, Lainey, breathe. She should move or say something to break the spell, but curiosity won, and her eyelids fluttered closed.

He shifted slightly, breaking the distance between them as his nose brushed against hers.

Her heart thumped wildly against her chest. Waiting. Anticipating the feeling of his lips firmly pressed against hers.

"Does anyone want more wine before I sit do— " Cheyenne let the sentence trail off.

Lainey's eyes flew open. Flustered, she moved away from Knox as far as the sofa would allow. She tucked loose strands of hair behind her ears. "How was your phone call?"

She couldn't focus on Cheyenne's response.

They'd almost kissed.

Knox wanted to kiss her.

And she would have let him.

––––––––

On Monday, Knox brought a large cup of coffee to a window-facing booth at the Wagon Wheel Café. This morning, he'd left early, as soon as Amos and Travis had plowed the driveway and Lainey headed out to the barn. He wasn't ready to see her after last night. He needed space to think. But now that he was away, all he could do was think about how close he'd been to kissing her. Until Cheyenne had walked in and ruined the moment.

It was for the best. Really, it was. That was how he had to see it. He had a job to do, and she was getting in his way. He'd wanted a promotion like this ever since he'd started at Mt. Point Development. If he didn't convince Lainey and her sisters to sell the land, he would lose the position. He'd be stuck with long hours and months of traveling. No time for a social life.

That didn't sit well. His chest ached with longing at the prospect of settling down, buying a home with someone, and starting a family.

Then again, what if the woman he was looking for was already right in front of him? Except there would be no happy ending for him and Lainey. Only one of them would get what they wanted in the end.

He leaned back in the booth and glanced out the window. The snow had stopped sometime in the middle of the night, and the sky was clear, exposing bright rays of sunshine. As a result, downtown was crowded. People rushed down the sidewalk, carrying bags full of Christmas gifts.

Knox grimaced. Another reminder that his deadline was fast approaching.

Georgia flitted to his table like a fairy. "Good morning, Cupcake." She paused, muttering to herself. "Nope, still not right. Would you like more coffee, Moon Pie?" She frowned, obviously not happy with that nickname either.

"I can never say no to caffeine." He held up his mug. "I'm curious. What's Lainey's nickname?"

"Bonbon."

"How did you come up with that?"

Georgia grinned. "Well, as a baby, she was plump and round. We always said she had thunder thighs. Cute as can be, though. You'd never be able to tell now. That girl skinnied up real fast. Then, as a toddler, it became quite apparent to me that she was gonna be one of those people who's a little hard on the outside but soft and sweet on the inside. Like a bonbon."

He returned her smile. The name fit Lainey

perfectly. She had a hard shell that was difficult to break through, but once he'd been around her more, she'd shown him how tender and compassionate she could be.

"No way." At a nearby table, the lawyer and the sheriff glared at each other. Their voices rose above the lively chatter. Floyd took off his thick glasses and wiped them with the bottom of his button-down shirt. "You're wrong, Hank. That memory of yours is as slippery as a wet fish between your fingers."

Hank folded his arms across his broad chest. The movement caused his badge to reflect the rays of sunlight pouring through the windows. "No, I'm not. I'll go to the station right now and check my reports if you really want me to."

Georgia cleared her throat and put one hand on her bony hip. "What are you two arguing about this time?"

"I told Floyd that Matthew Clemenson disappeared fifteen years ago when we had that real bad blizzard. Remember when the power went out for two weeks?" Hank continued on as if he hadn't asked a question. "When the power finally came back on, we all checked on each other to make sure everyone was safe. The mayor went to Matthew's house, but there was no sign of Matthew anywhere. No one ever saw him again."

Knox looked up from his screen. A missing person?

Floyd rubbed his earlobe. "No, no, no. It was twelve years ago. And it wasn't during a blizzard. It was a peaceful winter day. Matthew's boss came looking for him when he didn't show up for work."

Hank looked up at Georgia expectantly. "Which one of us is right?"

She gripped the handle of the coffeepot so tightly her knuckles turned white. "It was fourteen years ago in September. We had an early snowstorm that took everyone by surprise. The power was out for ten days. Matt disappeared shortly after that. And a lot of people went to his house looking for him." She spoke through clenched teeth. "I'm busy, so don't waste my time bothering me with your silly arguments." She quickly strode away from the table and disappeared behind the kitchen doors.

Knox poured creamer in his coffee. Scarlett had been right about Georgia being a rosebush. Apparently, she was in a thorny kind of mood today. Although, she'd seemed fine before Floyd and Hank had bothered her.

He turned toward the older men. "This Matthew guy … He didn't leave any evidence behind? No signs of a struggle or a note that he'd left on his own free will?"

Floyd nodded. "That's right. There were no footprints. No notes. No one has any idea what happened to him."

"Did you search for a body?"

"Yup. We searched for years. We didn't find a thing." Hank shoveled a large forkful of hash browns into his mouth. "I think a cougar got him. Or a wolf."

"There's no way he got eaten by a wild animal. He was too good of a hunter to die like that." Floyd put his thumbs beneath his suspenders and puffed out his thin chest. "If you want my opinion, he's still alive. I reckon he left and headed to California for a better life."

Hank scowled. "No one asked for your opinion, you old fool."

Knox chuckled. These two were hilarious. They could've acted in *Grumpy Old Men* and made a killing.

Scarlett rose from a table in the middle of the café where she'd been sitting with Evelyn and Sam eating breakfast. She sauntered over to Knox's booth dressed in tight jeans and a red low-cut sweater. She slid into the seat across from him and pointed a thumb at Floyd and Hank. "Are these two making up stories again?"

"We aren't doing anything of the sort. We—"

Hank was cut off by a voice coming through his dispatch radio. "Just pulled over a delivery truck full of cocaine and meth on Beartooth Highway."

The sheriff put the speaker up to his mouth. "I'll be right there." He got up so fast his chair skidded across the floor.

Floyd mumbled something unintelligible, something about having to pay for both meals.

Scarlett stared at the table for a minute, seemingly collecting her thoughts before she looked at Knox. "You seem like a good guy, so I'll be straight with you. The Evans sisters are wasting your time. It's not fair to you. I've seen firsthand how good Lainey is at getting what she wants."

Huh? "What are you talking about?"

Scarlett fidgeted with one of her large hoop earrings. "When Lainey and my brother were dating, Will thought they would get married one day. That might seem strange since they were so young and had only dated a year, but they'd been friends since we were little. Before he left for college, he assumed she'd want to make the long distance work, but then she dumped him out of the blue. Broke his heart."

Knox took a sip of coffee, contemplating Scarlett's concerns.

She rested her elbows on the table, exposing her ample cleavage. "I don't want you to get hurt."

He cupped his hands around his mug. Was this Scarlett's way of hitting on him? "Er, I appreciate that."

"Keep your eyes open, handsome." Without

waiting for his response, she walked back to the table to join her parents.

He shifted in the booth. Was it possible Scarlett was jealous he was spending so much time with Lainey? Or was she upset for other reasons?

Then again, how well did he really know Lainey?

Scarlett was right about one thing—Lainey hadn't shown any interest in selling the ranch. *Was* she stringing him along?

He finished his coffee, left cash on the table, and slid out of the booth. He had to get back to the ranch. Straighten things out and get the truth. Hopefully, his newfound concerns were wrong.

———

Lainey picked up a lead rope. It was time for Nutmeg to join up with her. The horse needed to view Lainey as the leader.

She moved forward slowly, walking in a circle as Nutmeg galloped around the perimeter of the fence. She made a clicking noise with her tongue and swung the rope down in front of Nutmeg's path to encourage the horse to change direction.

Nutmeg's eyes widened with surprise, and she changed course.

Lainey backed away, rounded the pen twice more,

then came closer to Nutmeg with the lead rope and swung it in front of the mare again.

Nutmeg's ears pulled back, her eyes alert, but not filled with surprised like she was the first time.

Lainey smiled. Progress.

After repeating the process several times, she turned her back on Nutmeg and stopped in the middle of the pen. She would wait to see if the horse would come to her, if the mare would acknowledge Lainey as the leader. *Come on, Mama.*

A minute later, hooves clip-clopped against the sand. Nutmeg trotted up behind Lainey and sniffed her shoulder.

Lainey faced the horse. "Good girl. You're so smart."

Quinn clapped and swung her legs over the fence, sitting on the highest board. "That was amazing. I hope you don't mind, but I recorded it."

"Why would I mind?"

"I think we should create a social media page for your business and post videos of you working with horses. You can use it for marketing."

Lainey scrunched her nose. "You mean strangers would be watching me?"

"Not strangers. People interested in hiring you."

"I haven't registered the business with the state of Montana yet. I should probably do that first."

She'd been dragging her heels. Making the business official felt wrong. Grandpa was supposed to be here for all these steps, and every time she moved forward with the business, her grief intensified and lessened her excitement. Preparing to start was just another reminder that he was gone.

Quinn continued, unaware of Lainey's feelings. "I'll just post videos and pictures on your personal sites. Make it less about marketing and more about your love for horses. Then once you have an LLC, I'll create the social media pages."

Lainey swallowed hard. When Grandpa died, she'd assumed she would have to start this business on her own. But her sisters had stepped up and helped. With ideas, the fundraiser, and now social media. It meant more than Cheyenne and Quinn would ever understand. "Go ahead and post the pictures and videos."

"Will do." Quinn crossed her ankles. "I had one other thing I wanted to talk to you about."

"What is it?"

Quinn pulled her long brown hair into a low ponytail that trailed down her slender back. "Don't get mad at me for saying this, but do you think you should be kissing Knox? I mean, he's trying to buy our land."

Lainey let go of the lead rope, allowing Nutmeg to move about the round pen. "How did you—"

"Cheyenne told me."

"I hope she told you that we *didn't* kiss."

"Yeah, but you *almost* did." Quinn hopped off the fence. "I get why you're falling for him. He's good-looking and charming. But as soon as he realizes we're not selling the land, he's out of here."

"I'm well aware of that," Lainey snapped. She'd just been grateful for her sisters a moment before. But why did their conversations get heated so often? Especially considering she was a grown woman who could make her own decisions. "You were the ones who wanted me to spend time with him, remember?"

"No one said anything about kissing him."

Lainey growled and threw her hands up in exasperation. "You shouldn't be kissing our ranch hand either. If it goes south with Travis, he'll probably quit. And then what?"

"Travis wouldn't quit. He enjoys working here. He likes working for you. He says you're doing a good job."

Her hands went limp at her sides. "Really?"

"Yeah." Quinn nodded. "Travis is a good guy. He even shows up to the arena to watch me practice. I don't think my coach likes it, but I do. It puts more pressure on me to do well."

"That *is* nice. Are you ready for the show?"

Quinn gave a confident nod, but she played with the end of her ponytail, giving her nerves away. "This will be the biggest one I've ever performed in.

My coach said about seven hundred thousand people go each year. This could be my ticket to the Olympics."

"You'll be great. You've been show jumping since you were little. Even before you could compete."

"Lainey!" Amos's yell carried across the open terrain.

She spun around as Travis sped across the land on a UTV with Amos riding beside him. As soon as they parked, Amos lifted his hand. A deep gash cut across his palm. Blood dripped down his forearm onto the frozen ground.

They both ran toward the men.

Lainey took off her jacket, then her flannel shirt. Good thing she'd worn long underwear today. She wrapped the flannel shirt around his injured hand.

Amos winced.

"Sorry. It'll stop the bleeding. What happened?" Lainey asked.

"Over on the west end, the fence was tipping, and the barbed wire was bent. We were using the unwinder machine, but apparently, the wire had been cut. It shot out of the machine and slashed my hand."

"Do you think someone tampered with our machine?"

"There's no doubt in my mind." Pain hung like a fog over each of Amos's words.

Her stomach twisted in knots as she tugged her coat back on. "Whoever did it wanted to hurt one of us."

Quinn gave a slow nod. "But why?"

"I wish I knew." She lifted her chin, hoping she looked calmer than she felt. "I should get you to the hospital, Amos."

As she walked with him toward her truck, a rush of adrenaline surged through her body. She had to find the saboteur before anyone else got hurt.

CHAPTER
Thirteen

BEHIND THE HOUSE, Knox set a thick log on top of a tree stump. He grabbed the ax, gripping it tightly in his hands. He could do this. He could cut kindling for the fire without slicing into his legs or cutting off his feet. He took a deep breath, swung, and nicked the edge of the wood. A small piece flew off toward the ground.

Well, that was embarrassing. At least no one else was around. Lainey was still at the hospital with Amos. Travis was rotating the cattle. Cheyenne and Quinn were in the kitchen with the sheriff, explaining what had happened this morning.

His plans to talk to Lainey would have to wait. They were down two people at the ranch, so Knox had asked Travis if he could help. The ranch hand mentioned the woodpile was low and asked Knox if he could handle an ax. Knox had said he could.

Now, he wasn't so sure. But he would figure it out. He lifted the ax, not holding it as high this time, and swung it toward the middle topside of the wood. Two uneven strips fell to the ground. He grinned. Despite the uneven sizes, there were, in fact, two pieces. He added them to the pile and swung again.

With each swing, he got a little better, his confidence rising. Weeks ago, he would've balked at the idea of chopping wood. But living on the ranch had changed his understanding of work. You couldn't stand around and think about whether you were qualified to do the job or not; you simply pitched in.

After thirty minutes, his body longed to stop. His fingers felt numb, and his shoulders ached. And yet, he kept going. Because if he stopped, he'd perseverate on Scarlett's warning. The fact that Lainey hadn't mentioned his offer *was* concerning, and he *did* deserve an update on her decision.

A car door slammed shut.

Was Lainey home? He put the ax away and tossed the last two wood pieces into the tall pile. He walked around the side of the house, his footsteps crunching through the snow.

Lainey trudged toward the barn. Her shoulders lowered and loose tendrils of hair clung to her face.

She caught sight of him, a weary smile spreading across her face.

He swallowed hard, her smile melting some of his prior concerns. She'd had a hard afternoon. He broke the distance between them and tucked the loose strands behind her ear. "How's Amos?"

"He needed stitches, but the doctor says the cut should heal quickly."

"Good. Are you OK?"

"Yeah." Her tone held little conviction.

"Why do you always pretend you're fine when you're not?"

She stiffened. "I am fine. Fine enough to get work done, anyway."

He squeezed her shoulders. "Why don't we go for a ride?" She always relaxed more while she rode. And it would be the perfect opportunity to bring up the offer. "Come on, please?" he asked.

"Ugh. You're relentless, you know that?"

He grinned. "Is that a yes?"

She nodded.

He helped tack up Jingle Bells and Rebel, and then they were on their way to the trail running along the river. They rode in silence for a while, stopping briefly to let the horses take a drink from the river.

He adjusted uneasily on the saddle. Part of him didn't want to bring up the offer, to make her day more complicated. But he had to stop wasting time. "Have you thought about my offer?"

"I'm still not sure what I want to do," she said quietly.

"What about Cheyenne and Quinn? What do they want?"

"I need to show you something." She led them to a connecting trail, going east up the mountain side.

He let out a frustrated sigh. "Where are we going?"

She glanced back for a moment, an unreadable expression on her face. "You'll see."

As they rode the horses onto higher ground, he gritted his teeth. All he wanted was an answer, and yet again, she had none. "Lainey, I deserve—"

"Look." She pulled on her horse's reins, stopping the mare as they neared a cliff.

He followed the direction of her gaze to the desert lowlands below. About a hundred mustangs roamed the expanse of land. His breath caught in his throat. The wild horses were unlike any he'd ever seen. They had narrow, deep chests with their front legs closer together than their hind legs; short, muscular backs with low-set tails; large expressive eyes; small ears; and wide foreheads that tapered into small muzzles, giving them V-shaped faces. "They're beautiful."

"They have Colonial Spanish-American heritage, which is why they have such distinctive features.

Many believe that these horses were stolen or traded to one of the Crow tribes, and the horses escaped to the Pryor Mountain Range."

"How many are there?"

"They average around a hundred and twenty. And they each have a name." She pointed at a brown mare with a black mane, who grazed near another horse with similar coloring. "That one is the lead mare, Broken Bow, and that's her daughter, Demure, next to her. They've always had a strong bond. They've been separated by stallions several times, and Broken Bow always finds her way back to her daughter."

He shook his head in awe. "I've never seen so many horses in one place."

"It's thirty-eight thousand acres of protected land. In fact, this was the first horse range established in the US."

"Wow." He couldn't say more on the topic, considering Vince had told him this fact during their first conversation about the ranch. He let silence settle between them once again, admiring the view before he tore his gaze away to look at Lainey. "Why are you showing me this?"

"Because you've made a point about me buying land somewhere else and building a new ranch. I want you to see that if I did that, I'd be losing all of this. Of course, I could use the public trails just like anyone else around here, but right now, I have a ranch that backs up to this area of land."

Dread anchored in the pit of his stomach. "Are you telling me you won't sell it, then?"

She noticeably swallowed. "No. I'm telling you that this decision is incredibly hard."

He gripped the round pommel connected to Rebel's saddle. "I understand, but I can't wait much longer. I need an answer."

A bush rustled behind them. Rebel's ears perked, and his large shoulders tensed. Both horses turned around to face the sound.

"What was that?" Knox asked.

Lainey squinted into the dense woods. "I don't know." She glanced down at Jingle Bells. "Stay still, girl."

His heart raced. If the horses got scared and backed up, they could fall off the cliff.

The bushes rustled again, followed by a faint moan.

"Something's hurt." Lainey hopped off Bells in one swift motion.

"What are you doing?" He spoke quietly, trying not to spook the horses or whatever animal was hiding in the underbrush.

She tiptoed closer, edging around the side of the bush.

He shook his head. Why did he bother? Of

course, Lainey wouldn't listen to him. Not when an animal could be hurt.

Reminding himself to breathe, he dismounted off Rebel. He followed Lainey a short distance, almost running into her when she stopped.

She cupped her hands over her cheeks. "Oh no. He's caught in a bear trap."

Knox rounded the corner and stood beside her, frozen.

A large gray wolf cub had his paw stuck in a metal trap chained to the ground. A foot away from the trapped cub was an even larger gray wolf with a distinctive white stripe of fur down its nose—most likely the cub's mother. When the mother caught sight of them, she rose from the ground, her sharp teeth bared.

The blood drained from his face. They had to get out of here. Maybe if they moved away slowly, posing no threat, the mother wouldn't come after them.

Whimpering, the cub looked up from his paw and tried to lunge forward at them. The chain linking the trap to the ground prevented him from going too far. All the while, his mother stayed rooted in place, a low growl escaping from her still bared teeth.

Jingle Bells and Rebel let out fearful neighs. They shifted their hooves in short, anxious movements, caught between the wolves and the cliff.

"Hold on to the horses," Lainey whispered. She slowly reached inside the saddle bag and pulled out a set of pliers. She slipped them into her back pocket. "I'm going to set the cub free."

Knox clutched the horses' reins, needing support to keep his shaking legs from buckling beneath him. Was she serious? Lainey had a big heart, but this was downright dangerous. "There's probably a wolf pack somewhere close by. And how are you going to get the cub free without the mother attacking us?" He spoke quietly, barely moving his mouth.

"I understand the risk." She paused for a moment, seemingly lost in thought. "I can get the mother to trust us."

"Can't we call someone instead? Like a wildlife employee?"

"We could. But it'll take them a while to get here and find this spot. If the cub keeps tugging on the trap, he'll do serious damage to his leg."

Knox resisted the urge to shake his head, too afraid to move. Once Lainey had her mind set, it was hard to change it. "Hold on while I tie the horses to a tree."

"No, don't. If the wolf attacks them, the horses wouldn't have any chance of getting away."

Adrenaline surged through his veins. If something went wrong, he would have to act fast. Swoop Lainey up in his arms, jump on Rebel, and gallop away, praying the wolf wouldn't follow or catch up to them.

Lainey set her hand on his forearm, her touch gentle and reassuring. "We can do this." She sent him a shaky smile.

So, she was nervous, after all.

"While I move toward the cub, talk to the mother in a calm, confident voice. Make sure you keep eye contact with her at all times."

He pulled his shoulders back, taking deep breaths before he spoke to the wolf. "It's OK. We're going to get your baby out. We want to help you."

Lainey moved off to the side, creeping closer to the cub.

He almost glanced her way, simultaneously horrified and in awe of her courage.

"Soon, your baby will be free, and you can go back to your pack." He kept his tone even but thinking of the nearby pack made his insides quake.

Lainey stepped on a branch, and it cracked in two. She stopped and froze. She was close enough now that the cub could bite her.

The young wolf stepped back, glaring at Lainey with menace. The movement must have caused him pain because he immediately lowered his body to the ground and whimpered. His mother repositioned herself right next to her baby, leaving no space between them.

Knox's heart rate spiked again. Before he could think of something else to say, Lainey slowly lowered herself onto the snow-covered ground and sat.

The mother cocked her head to the side, as if she was surprised by the human sitting near her.

Lainey sat motionless, showing the wolves that she meant them no harm. The woods were eerily quiet as time seemed to stand still. The only indication of its passing was the sun lowering in the sky, causing an orange hazy glow through the trees.

Eventually, the mother wolf lay down. She kept her head up, her gaze only wavering from Lainey to glance at Knox.

Lainey must have taken that as a good sign. She gradually pulled the pliers out of her pocket and set them in front of the wolves.

The mother sniffed the metal instrument. When the animal lifted her head, no longer curious, Lainey removed the pliers from the ground and edged as close as she could to the cub. The young wolf looked at his mother, their silent communication apparent but not decipherable.

Knox held his breath. What was the cub saying to his mother?

With the cub's head turned, Lainey quickly used the pliers to compress the levels on the trap.

The jaws of the trap sprung open.

The cub lifted his paw out. His mother licked the injury, cleaning off the blood.

Lainey stood and tiptoed backward. The cub looked up and opened his mouth, saliva hanging off his sharp teeth as he let out a growl.

It would only take seconds for him to run at Lainey and attack.

Her face went stark white. She kept moving backward, closer to Knox.

The mother finished cleaning the wound, rose, and started to walk away. She waited for the cub to start following her before she turned her head, gave Lainey and Knox one last glance, then disappeared into the woods.

Tension unraveled from Knox's limbs. He loosened his grip on the horses and pulled Lainey tight against him. He cupped her head with his hand, holding her close to his chest.

Her body trembled as she bound her arms around his lower back. "I can't believe we just did that."

He moved his hand to her cheek, stroking her soft skin with his thumb. "You were so brave."

"I couldn't have done it without your help."

A lump the size of a golf ball formed in his throat. What if something bad had happened to her? Without another thought, he leaned forward and closed his eyes. His lips brushed against hers.

She didn't react, her lips unmoving. Her arms fell to her sides.

He opened his eyes and straightened to his full height. Was she angry? He opened his mouth to apologize but was cut off by her lips fitting firmly against his.

She draped her arms around his neck. Her fingers threaded his hair as her lips parted for a deeper kiss.

Heat pooled low in his stomach. Electric tingles shot across his skin. She tasted every bit as good as he'd imagined. Sweet, like the peppermints she so often kept in her pockets.

A low moan escaped from her throat.

If their lips weren't locked, he would've smiled. She wanted him as badly as he wanted her.

He shuddered, losing all track of time as he lost himself in her.

Finally, it was Lainey who mumbled something incoherent against his mouth and slowly drew away. Her lips glistened from the kiss, full and swollen. "That was …" Her cheeks turned an adorable shade of crimson.

She didn't need to finish the sentence. It had been amazing.

Rebel and Jingle Bells let out long *neighs*.

Lainey scanned the darkening woods. "It's getting late. Wolves aren't our only predators, especially at night. We need to get back."

He nodded reluctantly. All too soon, reality would hit, and he'd be forced to confront what had just happened between them.

––––––––

The moon guided their way, creating eerie shadows along the path. An owl hooted from the treetops above. Winged creatures—most likely bats—made whooshing sounds as they took flight to catch prey.

Lainey trembled. Not only from the danger they'd just encountered with the wolves but from the kiss.

Oh, that kiss.

She felt dizzy from it. It almost didn't feel real. Like a dream she'd imagined. The kiss had been *that* good. Maybe the best kiss she'd ever had.

Definitely, the best kiss she'd ever had.

Not that she should dwell on it.

It shouldn't have happened. In a moment of weakness, she'd given in to temptation.

Rebel stumbled over a dead branch that had fallen on the trail. Knox held on tight as the horse regained his balance.

"It's too dark. The horses could get hurt," Lainey said. "I think we should set up camp for the night. I always carry supplies with me in the saddle pack, just in case."

He raised an eyebrow. "You're not trying to take advantage of me, are you?"

She gave a nervous giggle, resisting the urge to smack her forehead. What was happening to her? Since when did she giggle? She wasn't the type to go all googly for a guy. "Of course not."

"Isn't the shack a little farther down this path?"

"You mean the haunted shack?"

Smirking, he puffed out his chest. "Don't worry, if any ghosts show up, I'll protect you."

She rolled her eyes.

"In all seriousness, it'll be warmer in there."

Lainey bit her bottom lip. Staying anywhere with Knox overnight was a really bad idea. But he had a point. The temperature had dropped significantly since they'd started this trip. The air was so cold it bit into the exposed skin on her face. "Fine." She reached down to grab a flashlight from the saddle pack. "Come on, Bells, let's go." She pressed her legs into the horse's sides and pulled the reins on the left, guiding the mare off the trail and into the woods.

Fifteen minutes later, they stopped in front of the shack. Her eyebrows furrowed together. "Something's wrong. I smell smoke." She shined the flashlight up above the chimney. Clouds of smoke billowed from the top.

"It looks like someone recently extinguished a

fire." Knox dismounted and peered down at his boots. "Shine the flashlight at the ground."

Footprints led from the shack. Fear twisted knots inside her stomach. Saving the wolf cub had been the scariest thing she'd ever done. And yet, knowing someone was out here, on their property, was just as frightening. Where was the person now? Inside the shack, or somewhere nearby watching them?

She dismounted off Jingle Bells and reached for her pistol.

Knox stared at the gun. "You had that on you the whole time we were with the wolves?"

"Yeah. I also have a rifle. I would've used a gun if I had to, but we were trying to *save* the wolf, not harm it."

He pinched the bridge of his nose. It looked like he wanted to say more, but his jaw tightened instead.

If she wasn't so frightened, she would've laughed. "I'll go in first." Holding the pistol with clammy hands, she cautiously approached the shack. The door creaked as she opened it wide and stepped inside. "If anybody's in here, you better come out now. I have a gun."

No one responded.

Keeping the gun pointed forward, she walked through the cabin with Knox at her heels, using the flashlight to guide their search. With every step, her leg muscles tightened, ready to flee at any moment.

The living room was empty, except for a rocking chair sitting on top of a bear fur rug.

A matching handcrafted table and chair were in the vacant kitchen.

Next, she approached the bedroom. Her heart pounded in her chest. As the only closed-off room, this would be the one space where someone would be able to hide easily. She stepped inside, finding another bear fur rug and a bed.

Dread anchored to the pit of her stomach. Whoever the occupant was, they'd been here for a while.

She climbed the stairs to the loft, again finding no one. She finally let out a breath and lowered the gun. "We're alone. For now. I'm going to bring the horses inside. It'll be cramped, but they'll be safer with us, in case someone is still close by."

"Makes sense," Knox said. "I'll try to get a fire started."

She brought the horses in and fed them carrots and water as they stood side by side in the entryway. Exhaustion crawled through her weary limbs, but she couldn't sit still. Instead, she paced the floor. "I can't believe this. Who knows how long someone has been staying here? For all we know, it could be the same person sabotaging the ranch. This is the perfect location to oversee our day-to-day lives without getting caught."

A flicker of light brightened in the fireplace. Knox bent over and blew on the embers, creating a growing flame. He turned to look at her and held out his hand. "Come here. You need to rest."

She stopped pacing and walked to his side, letting him pull her to the ground. Warmth from the fire blanketed the air around them, thawing her skin.

He wrapped his arm around her waist. "Better?"

Lainey nodded. Adrenaline still pumped through her veins, but Knox was right. She needed to relax. She closed her eyes and rested her head on his shoulder.

"I need to tell you something."

Her eyelids fluttered open. "What is it?"

"Remember the first day you took me riding?"

"Yeah …"

"As we were riding away from this area, I thought I saw a face in the window. I didn't mention it because I thought I was seeing things after you'd told me the ghost story. But now, it's obvious that it was a real person."

She lifted her head, gazing into Knox's eyes. "This is bad. How am I supposed to run the ranch and keep my family safe? We still have no idea who's behind all of this, or why." A tear slipped down her cheek. "My grandpa would know what to do. He always did."

"Don't be so hard on yourself. You're doing a

great job." Knox caught her tear with his thumb and wiped it away. "We'll call the sheriff as soon as we get back tomorrow."

"What if the person comes back tonight?" she asked quietly.

He was silent for a moment before he spoke. "I don't think that will happen. With the fire going, it's pretty clear that we're still here. They must not want a confrontation, or else they would've stayed when they heard us coming."

"That's true."

"I'll grab the blankets from the bedroom, and we can lie by the fire to keep it going. I don't mind taking the first shift." When he returned with the blankets, they kicked off their boots and set them near the fire. He bunched one of blankets into a pile near their heads for a makeshift pillow.

She almost smiled. It was nice to be taken care of for once.

As soon as she lay down, he pulled the other blanket over their bodies. He settled in behind her, pressing his body against hers. His foot gently rubbed against the arches of her feet.

Her breathing steadied. Knox had a way of calming her, much like a horse's ability to regulate a steady heartbeat. She'd never connected with a man, or any other human, like she did with him.

Which wasn't good. Soon, he'd be gone and out of her life forever.

But she'd worry about that tomorrow. Because right now, with his body wrapped around hers, it felt surprisingly right.

CHAPTER
Fourteen

THE NEXT DAY, Knox and Lainey had woken up at sunrise and made the trek back to Lost Canyon Ranch. Cheyenne and Quinn had come running out of their bedrooms, relieved to see that they were safe. Quinn had tried calling multiple times, but her calls hadn't gone through.

After eating breakfast, Knox escaped to the loft to take a short nap while Lainey called the sheriff. Best-case scenario, Hank would find fingerprints during his investigation, and he'd be able to identify the person inhabiting the shack.

Knox awoke two hours later and rolled his shoulders, his muscles screaming in protest. His whole body ached after sleeping on the hardwood floor last night. He couldn't call it a bad night, though, not when he'd spent it with Lainey.

He stumbled out of bed, a groggy smile spreading across his face. He'd finally broken down her walls. She'd finally let him comfort her.

Where was she now? No way had she taken a nap like him. She was probably outside, doing chores. He strolled across the loft and peered out the window. Lainey walked toward the barn, then she stopped, looked up, and waved. Heat crept into his cheeks.

Hiding his embarrassment, he waved and moved away from the window. Where did they go from here? To pursue anything further would be foolish. As soon as she signed over the land, he'd go back to Seattle. Sure, he'd visit to check on the progress, but she wouldn't be living on the ranch.

And if she didn't sign over the land, he'd go home with a failure on his resume and no promotion. And who would he have to blame? Her.

He shook his head. That was too harsh. This was *her* land. And the longer he stayed at the ranch, the harder it was to imagine her somewhere else.

He had to admit that she was getting to him.

But he couldn't change course now. He had to stick to the plan, acquire the land, and get the promotion he'd worked hard for.

Unease strangled any enthusiasm before it could take root.

Sighing, he changed into jeans and a sweatshirt, catching sight of his reflection in the mirror. His typically styled hair hung low on his forehead. Two days' worth of stubble covered his jaw. Jeans and sweat-shirts had never been his style, even on weekends. What was happening to him?

It wasn't just Lainey getting to him; it was life on a ranch.

He needed to get a grip.

An email notification popped up on his phone. He picked it up off the dresser and clicked on his emails.

Knox,

G. S. has offered to meet with you. Go to Lone Star Saloon in Red Lodge at noon. Don't mess this up.

—Vince

He let out a quiet whoop. *Yes.* This could be the edge he needed to give him the upper hand. And he couldn't meet the client looking like this. He quickly undressed and headed for the shower. Time to pull himself back together.

An hour later, he left the ranch without seeing Lainey. She was in the barn, probably checking on Cocoa.

At noon, he entered the Lone Star Saloon. Colorful Christmas lights were strung across dark walls, and holiday music played softly from the surround-sound speakers. A group of white-haired men sat at a table playing cards. The bar was mostly empty, except for a redheaded woman sitting at a booth near the far side of the restaurant. She sat with her back to the door. He tilted his head to the side. It couldn't be … could it?

Just then, she turned and looked at him.

Scarlett.

His eyes widened. No way. So, she wasn't jealous. She was invested in the project, and she'd wanted him to stay focused. It made sense now.

He strode over to the table and sat down across from her. "You're G. S.?"

She nodded. "Georgia's called me Ginger Snap ever since I was a little girl."

Ginger Snap. Of course, he'd heard Georgia refer to Scarlett by that nickname. But Georgia used so many nicknames it was hard to keep them straight. If only he had picked up on that detail sooner.

A waitress wearing a Santa hat stopped by their booth. "What can I getcha?" she asked, exposing a large wad of bubble gum.

"I'll have a whiskey sour," Scarlett said.

"I'll have a Coke or Pepsi."

Scarlett handed the waitress some cash. "He'll have what I'm having."

"Oh, I don't need … It's a little early …"

Scarlett waved her hand dismissively. "You wouldn't let a lady drink alone, would you?"

Okay, then.

After the waitress walked away, Scarlett leaned forward. "I want to make one thing clear before I say anything else. Besides Vince Richfield, no one can know I'm the one who wants to buy Lost Canyon Ranch. I haven't told my parents, and until the deal is done, I don't want them involved."

"Why not? They're excited about a dude ranch resort."

"I'm the only girl out of five kids." She lifted her chin. "My parents have always babied me. This is my chance to prove myself. But I want to do it on my own, without their help."

"I see."

The waitress returned with their drinks.

"Thanks," he said.

Scarlett held up her glass and clinked it against his. "Cheers."

He took a drink. The whiskey burned as it slid down his throat. "Why did you agree to meet with me after all this time?"

"I wasn't anticipating the deal would take this long." She sat up straighter and pushed her shoulders back. "When I first contacted Mr. Richfield, he said you were one of their best. That's why he sent you. Said you close deals faster than anyone."

He shifted in the booth. "That's usually true. The Evans sisters—"

"I don't want any excuses. If you can't convince them to sell, then I'll have to ask your boss to send someone else."

"I can handle this."

"Can you? From where I'm sitting, Lainey is clouding your vision. I've already warned you about her. She's not someone you want to be involved with." Scarlett avoided his gaze as she downed the rest of her drink. "She'll chew you up and spit you out just like she did with my brother."

Knox squeezed the back of his neck. She had broken Will's heart, but was that her fault? Sometimes, things didn't work out. Was Scarlett's animosity truly warranted? "Why did you choose Lost Canyon Ranch as the location for your resort?"

Scarlett signaled to the waitress to bring her another drink. "It's the biggest plot of land in Cherry Creek. It backs up to the mountains with easy access to the trails and the river."

"Ah." Her word choice, or lack thereof, was interesting. She hadn't mentioned easy access for *guests*. If she was about to run a resort, wouldn't that be her first response?

Then again, why would she need easy access to the trails and river for herself? That didn't make sense either.

"Why do you want to run the resort?" he asked.

"It has great potential." Scarlett nodded at the

waitress, who set the whiskey sour on the table. "There's nothing like it around for miles."

His jaw tightened. That was her reasoning? The way she said it, so matter-of-factly, she could've been talking about the weather. He'd worked with plenty of businesspeople, and most of them had a vision and enthusiasm for the project. For someone who wanted to own a business, it didn't sound like she cared about the resort.

"Have you considered a different location?" The question was out before he could stop it.

She finally met his gaze again, anger flaring in her green eyes. "Of course, I've considered all the options. I've been thinking about this for years. Lost Canyon Ranch is the best location." She pointed a long, manicured finger at him. "If you aren't capable of getting me this land, I'll find another company to represent me."

"No. Don't do that." He shook his head. "I'll find a way."

"You'd better. I want this deal done." She chugged her drink, rose from the booth, and strode out of the bar.

He raked both hands through his hair, disheveling the styled strands. Something was off with Scarlett's responses. He couldn't put his finger on it, though.

And that wasn't the only problem. Lainey would

be devastated if she knew Scarlett, of all people, wanted to own her ranch. If this deal went through, Lainey wouldn't want anything to do with him afterward.

———

Lainey knelt on the rug in front of the fireplace and opened a box of Christmas tree ornaments. Two mugs of steaming hot chocolate rested on an end table by the couch. Fresh pine scented the room, thanks to Amos, who'd cut and trimmed a tree this afternoon. "A Holly Jolly Christmas" by Burl Ives floated through the living room from a playlist on the TV.

Cheyenne hummed along to the music as she stood on a step stool and wove silver garland around the branches.

Lainey frowned. If only her sister's good mood would rub off. Decorating the tree was one of her favorite holiday pastimes. Grandpa would cut it down, then he would spend the following day decorating with her while Mom and Quinn baked cookies. They'd sing along to the music, his voice in perfect pitch and hers way off-tune. But today, she didn't have the heart to sing about A Holly Jolly Christmas. Instead, "Where Are You, Christmas?" felt much more appropriate.

Earlier this morning, Hank Guthrie had called to report his findings after inspecting the shack. Like she'd suspected, someone had been living there for a while. The occupant had left behind rotten meat and fecal matter. Hank found fingerprints on the doorknobs, but unfortunately, the prints didn't match any others on record.

They were back to ground zero with a saboteur on the loose.

The ranch was falling apart without Grandpa. Car accidents. Broken fences. Injured ranch hands. Even though none of it was her fault, it had happened on her watch.

Knox was also a big part of her dampening mood. Ever since they'd kissed four days ago, he'd been different. Distant. He'd spent every day in town, away from the ranch. He always came back for dinner, but he was more reserved, lost in thought.

There could only be one reason: he regretted kissing her.

She picked up her hot chocolate and took a sip. The hot liquid burned, much like the sting of his rejection. It was stupid, really. She shouldn't be this affected by his actions. Their relationship could never go anywhere.

Maximus curled up next to her as she untangled several paper clips that were attached to ornaments. What if she and Knox had met under different circumstances? What if Mt. Point Development didn't want to buy her ranch? Would he try to pursue her? Would he want to kiss her again?

There were too many what-ifs to consider.

Best not to think about it.

She finished untangling the ornaments and laid them out on the rug. Not thinking about Knox only led to other concerns. Like the court hearing tomorrow. Worst-case scenario, Evelyn won the case, Lainey's reputation would suffer, and no one would want to hire her to train their horses.

"What do you think?" Cheyenne asked.

"Huh?"

"Do you want to have a theme?" Cheyenne pushed the step stool aside. "We could have a Santa-themed tree. I found a ton of Santa ornaments. Some look brand new like they were never taken out of their store-bought boxes."

Lainey shook her head. "If we have a theme, then we can't use the other ornaments. Grandpa loved seeing our handmade crafts and retelling the stories that went with them."

"Most of them are made out of paper." Cheyenne picked up a red-and-white Santa bauble in her hand. "And covered in messy paint."

"They're special." Lainey found a green sparkly picture frame made out of popsicle sticks that bordered a photo of Grandma and Grandpa's wedding. "See?"

Cheyenne sighed. "They make the tree look tacky."

Tacky. Was that what her sister thought of their memories?

"I don't even know how to respond to that," she said flatly.

Cheyenne hung the light-up Santa in the middle of the tree, turned, and put her hands on her hips. "You are so frustrating."

"Is that so?"

"Yeah, actually it is. Be honest, you don't like my idea because it's different from what you normally do."

Lainey lifted her chin. "There's nothing wrong with being traditional."

"The problem is you don't want to change *anything*. Not in the house or the barn or the ranch. Some things *need* to change."

"You sound like Knox," Lainey mumbled.

"Well, he's right." On the floor beside her, Cheyenne's phone lit up with a call. Her shoulders went limp. She swallowed and pressed *Ignore Call*.

"Was that Damian again?"

"Yup." Cheyenne reached for her hot chocolate and took a sip. White foam stuck to her upper lip.

She wiped it away with a napkin, her expression darkening.

"Why is he still calling you? Doesn't he understand that it's over?"

Cheyenne crumpled the napkin in her hands. "He wants to change my mind."

What had her sister ever seen in Damian? When he'd visited Lost Canyon Ranch, all he'd done was boast about *his* family's ranch in Tennessee—their state-of-the-art equipment, the hundreds of thousands of acres that made up their property between their deed and leases, their extensive barn with forty horse stalls … He'd gone on and on the entire weekend. Instead of getting to know Cheyenne's family.

By the last day of the visit, Lainey couldn't take it anymore. She'd told him that he was no longer welcome and shouldn't ever come back.

Although Damian had deserved it, Lainey's demand had significantly affected her relationship with Cheyenne. "I'm sorry for what happened when Damian was here. I was upset because he didn't seem to have your best interests at heart."

Cheyenne pressed her eyelids shut, her long lashes briefly gracing her cheeks before she opened her eyes. "You were right, though. I didn't see it back then. When I first started dating Damian, I fell hard for him. He was charming and well-liked by a lot of 'it' people in Nashville. He said I had great potential in country music. It felt so good to finally have someone believe in me that I didn't see all the red flags along the way."

Lainey moved boxes off to the side and sat cross-legged near her sister. Maximus followed her and sat in her lap. "Finally? We loved hearing you sing."

"That's not the same as believing in me. None of you truly understood my passion, except for Grandpa. He's the one who inspired my love for music in the first place."

"It was hard for me to understand why you wanted a life that was different from how we grew up. And when you moved away without saying goodbye, it felt a lot like the day Dad left." Though the words popped out of her mouth without thought, they were true. That was what had been bothering her all along.

All this time, she'd been harboring resentment toward Cheyenne when her feelings stemmed from deeper wounds that still hadn't healed.

Cheyenne noticeably swallowed. "I'm sorry I made you so upset. Especially after what Dad did to us."

"It's OK. You didn't mean to. I see that now." Lainey squeezed her sister's hand. Discussing Dad caused a heavy weight to settle in her chest. She needed to turn this conversation around before she got too emotional. "What are you going to do about

Damian? You can't let this continue, with him calling all the time. You need space to move on."

Cheyenne blew out a deep breath. "I need to talk to him one last time, and then I'm changing my number." Moisture filled her eyes. "He took most of my money. I didn't realize it until the other day when I offered to financially support your business."

"He took your money? How was he able to do that?"

"He convinced me to share an account with him so he could easily pay for industry-related expenses." A sob escaped Cheyenne's throat. Her tears flowed freely now, falling quickly down her ivory skin. "I feel so stupid. You saw through him right away, and I didn't."

Lainey leaned forward and wrapped Cheyenne in a hug. "Don't say that. You're not stupid. You were in love with him."

Maximus hopped out of her lap and licked Cheyenne's tears.

"I can't believe I'm saying this, but I'm glad to be home." Cheyenne rubbed behind Maximus's ears. "It's exactly where I needed to be this Christmas."

Lainey smiled. "I'm glad you are too." She glanced over at the tree with mostly barren branches. "Should we finish decorating?"

Cheyenne nodded. "Definitely."

Lainey reached inside the box full of Santa ornaments. "These are pretty cute. Maybe we could ask Amos to cut a smaller tree, reserved for just our handmade ornaments."

A slow, shaky smile spread across Cheyenne's face. "That's a great idea."

Lainey hung the Santas in various places. Despite the distraction, an unsettling feeling creeped into her gut. Cheyenne had fallen for Damian, a man so charming that her sister hadn't questioned his motives.

Could Knox's charm be *her* downfall? It hurt to consider that, but maybe she needed to consider the idea more. He'd been upfront and honest about why he was here, hadn't he? That was what he said.

Was it possible he was keeping something from her, that his motives weren't as they seemed either?

CHAPTER
Fifteen

THE DOORBELL CHIMED, sounding louder than normal without anyone else around. Lainey, Cheyenne, and Quinn had left two hours ago to attend the mediation at the courthouse.

Knox saved the latest draft of his designs for the resort and rose from the kitchen table. "Coming!" He walked to the mudroom and opened the front door, then immediately took a step back.

Vince stood on the front porch wearing a black suit and tie and carrying a briefcase. His immaculate boss looked out of place standing on the decrepit porch.

Knox must have looked the same way to Lainey when he'd first arrived. No wonder she'd been put off by him.

He shifted his weight from one foot to the other. "Vince. I wasn't expecting you."

"It's amazing how chatty people in small towns can be. All I had to do was go to the Wagon Wheel Café and ask about you. I spoke to a Gina, no, maybe it was Gemma."

"Georgia," Knox corrected.

"Yes, that's it. She told me you were here." Vince's questioning gaze scanned down to Knox's bare feet and then up to his sweatpants and T-shirt. "Is there something going on that you haven't told me about?"

His Adam's apple bobbed up and down. Too much to explain. He'd start with the most obvious. "I've been staying at the ranch."

Vince loosened the knot of his tie. "Are you going to invite me in? It's freezing outside."

He looked out the door, past Vince's shoulder. Lainey and her sisters could be back from court any minute. But he couldn't send his boss away. It would be rude. "Come on in. Follow me." He led Vince to the kitchen table. "Can I get you anything to drink?"

"No, thanks." Vince took a seat and set his briefcase next to the hardwood chair. "Why aren't you at a hotel? Didn't Irene make a reservation for you in Red Lodge?"

"Yes, but the granddaughters offered to let me stay at their ranch."

"Why would they do that?"

He almost chuckled because it *was* crazy that they'd asked him to stay, but nothing about Vince's impromptu visit was funny. "People in Cherry Creek take hospitality to a whole new level."

Vince leaned forward and rested his elbows on the table, fixing Knox with a hard stare. "You do remember why you're here, right? This isn't so you can play rancher and shack up with one of the local cowgirls."

Ouch. "That's not what I'm doing, sir." Knox pulled back his shoulders. He needed Vince to trust his business instincts. "Staying at the ranch has benefits. I've gotten to know the women and have a better understanding of what would get them to sell. I have daily access to the ranch. I know the land well by now. I've also drafted several design options for the resort. I was just working on one if you want to see it."

"Of course."

Knox turned the tablet toward his boss. "This house could be the lobby where Scarlett can stay and do check-ins and check-outs. The rest of the buildings could be torn down, replaced with four or five family-sized cabins. Once we make the deal, I'll see if Scarlett wants kitchenettes inside each cabin or if she plans to prepare meals in this house and bring them to guests." As he spoke, a lump formed in his throat. The idea of building a resort was still exciting, but tearing down the ranch? The prospect didn't hold the same luster it had when he'd first arrived.

"These are great designs, but if we don't own the land, it won't matter."

"Sir, I can see why you're concerned. I've handled this project in an unorthodox way by staying at the property we'd like to buy. But I'll prove to you that my actions are worth it in the end."

"I sure hope so." Vince moved to the edge of his chair. "Let me remind you that you have a rare chance at Mt. Point Development to become the vice president. There are many developers who would kill to have my position. Before you left, I thought you were one of them."

"I am." He spoke the words so quickly that he barely gave any thought to his response. He had wanted the position. More than anything. But now? Did he still want to settle down in Seattle? The bigger question was, did he want to say goodbye to Lainey for good?

No, definitely not.

And yet, buying and selling property was part of his job. A job he enjoyed. A job he strived to be good at.

Vince opened his briefcase and pulled out a small stack of papers neatly clipped together. "This is a new contract. We're offering five hundred and twenty thousand over the property value, which is twenty thousand more than the original offer. You have one more week to convince them to sell. If you can't do it, I will." He rose to a standing position. "I'm working remotely while I stay at the hotel in Red Lodge. If you need me, that's where I'll be. I can see myself out." He left the house without another word.

Knox rubbed his temples. He'd let Lainey get in the way. He needed to buck up, get the Evans women to see his perspective, and do what he came to do.

———

Lainey trudged out of the courthouse; her shoulders stooped. Dark ominous clouds moved across the sky, threatening snow. She should be in a hurry to get back to the ranch and prepare for the storm, but she wasn't.

During the mediation, Evelyn claimed to have prolonged neck pain, which resulted in physical therapy. She also brought up Tori's broken arm and requested that her granddaughter receive money for the emotional damage done that day.

Lainey presented the vet's findings, which showed that Jingle Bells had digested cocaine. But it did little good since someone from *her* ranch was most likely the one to expose the horse to cocaine. As much as she wanted to argue that point, she had no proof of who else might have done it.

In the end, Lainey agreed to thirty thousand dollars for physical and emotional damages to Evelyn and Tori. That was better than the hundred thousand Evelyn had asked for. But it was enough to drain the money Grandpa had given her, plus some of her savings. It would be years before she could get the horse training business up and running.

Cheyenne sighed. "I wish I could help."

Lainey dipped her chin to her chest. "It just wasn't meant to be. Maybe one day." It wasn't how she actually felt, but what else was there to say?

Quinn started the truck's engine as they piled in but made no attempt to drive away. She gripped the steering wheel and took a deep breath. "I can't believe I'm saying this, but there is another option."

Lainey stared at her lap. "What?"

"*If* we obtain the ranch, we could take Knox's offer. You would have enough money to pay off Evelyn, buy a ranch, and start the business. You wouldn't have to wait."

Sitting in the passenger's seat, Lainey looked at Quinn. The sister who'd always supported her. The one who loved the ranch as much as she did. The person who would never suggest giving it up unless she saw no other alternative. "You might be right," she said quietly.

Grandpa's dreams—her dreams—were more important than the location of their ranch. Yes, it was their home, the place where they'd grown up, but that was the past. The future mattered too. Training horses was what she was meant to do. She felt it to her very core, the essence of her being.

She looked at her sisters. "Do you both support this decision?"

"Yes," they said in unison.

Cheyenne nodded for emphasis. "Pursuing my singing career was the most liberating experience of my life. I want that for you. Besides Grandpa, I've never met anyone as good with horses as you are."

Moisture built in Lainey's eyes. She blinked the oncoming tears away and sniffled.

"It'll be hard at first, but it's for the best … right?" Quinn's lips trembled. She held Lainey's gaze, her expression full of uncertainty like when she was a little girl asking if Lainey wanted to play with her.

Lainey sniffled again. "Yeah. It's for the best."

Her chest rose and fell, defeat settling in like a heavy blanket. She would lose her home. Lost Canyon Ranch would no longer be her family's ranch. She'd have to start over.

Big, wet snowflakes dropped from the sky, splattering against the windshield.

"We better get home before the storm hits."

Quinn reversed out of the parking spot and pulled onto the road.

Lainey leaned her head against the cold window. Now that the decision had been made, her body felt numb. She couldn't afford to feel anything more, not yet.

———

Knox ran a brush over Rebel's body, gently running the bristles along the horse's neck, back, and thighs. Rebel closed his big eyes, clearly enjoying the grooming session. After Vince had left the ranch, Knox went straight to the barn. He'd been too worked up to do anything else. And being around Rebel meant that the horse would work his magic by steadying Knox's heart rate.

So far, it was working. Mostly. But his mind still had the conversation with Vince on repeat. This was not what he'd pictured when he'd taken on this project. He'd planned on it being a success. Not a dead end. Not a roadblock for his career.

Car doors slammed shut, followed by footsteps, then the front door creaked open.

He frowned. It wasn't like Lainey to head into the house first instead of the barn. That wasn't a good sign. Had Evelyn gotten what she'd wanted? Would Lainey's reputation suffer? His chest pinched at the thought. The urge to comfort her was overwhelming. Ever since their kiss five days ago, he'd tried to keep his distance. As if distance could change his feelings for her. But he had to try.

And yet, if she was hurting, he had to make her feel better.

He finished brushing Rebel, led the horse back into his stall, and slid the lock in place. "I'll see you later, buddy. OK?"

Rebel extended his neck over the door and pressed his muzzle against Knox's cheek.

Knox ran his fingers through the gelding's mane. "Are you trying to butter me up for a treat?" He pulled a carrot out of his coat pocket and placed it on his palm. "Oh, all right. Here you go." The hairs from Rebel's muzzle tickled his hand as the horse gobbled up the vegetable. "You're a good boy." He rubbed his hand against his jeans, rubbing off the slobber.

The movement almost made him laugh. Since when had slobber stopped bothering him? When had he started talking to horses or taking refuge in the barn?

This broken-down building had once disgusted him. The stench repugnant.

Living on a ranch had changed him.

Living with Lainey had changed him even more.

He left the barn as snowflakes swirled through the air. A blast of brisk wind blew across the open terrain, stinging his face. Shivering, he hurried inside the house.

Lainey sat alone at the kitchen table with her arms crossed as she stared at his tablet.

Dread weaseled its way into his gut. In his haste to get out of the house, he'd left the tablet on the table. The design program had been left open. The new contracts were also on the table. Had Lainey seen those too?

"I can explain," he said.

Her lips drew into a thin line. "Why do you already have designs for the resort when we haven't accepted your offer yet? Are you that confident you'll convince me? Or were you planning to bulldoze us into accepting your offer if we declined?"

"No. I wanted to be prepared if you did. That's it."

"Even if I sell you the land, do you understand how difficult it is to look at these designs? To see my barn, my garage, my shed, my chicken coop, all torn down? To see my house turned into some kind of shared living space with a lobby?"

He opened his mouth, then closed it. Had she just said *if* I sell you the land? Was she close to accepting? He gripped the back of a kitchen chair. "I made a mistake. I shouldn't have left my work sitting out. I was showing the designs to my boss."

Her forehead creased. "Your boss was in my house?"

"Vince showed up unannounced. I had no idea he was planning to come to Montana. He came here to tell me that if I can't convince you, he'll step in."

Her downturned face was pale. Using her thumbnail, she picked at a piece of dried food on the table and mumbled something incoherent. "Is that why there's a new contract?"

She had seen it, after all. The fact that she'd mentioned the designs first instead of the money was surprising, and yet, Lainey didn't care about money, she cared about her home.

Silence settled over the kitchen. Above the sink, the rooster-themed clock ticked, signaling the minutes passing.

This was it. The moment when one of them would give in. "What do you think of the contract?"

She dropped her hands in her lap and met his gaze. "We'll accept your offer … if we can." She winced as she spoke, the emotional pain of the decision written all over her face.

Knox froze, unable to move, unable to process his own conflicting emotions. Relief and satisfaction were nowhere to be found. Not with Lainey sitting directly in front of him, her anguish radiating from her slumped shoulders to her lowered chin to the quiver of her lips. Then her exact wording hit him. "What do you mean by 'if we can'?"

She tucked a strand of hair behind her ear. "We don't technically own it right now."

He gripped the top of the kitchen chair harder. "You told me it was yours," he said through clenched teeth.

"The day we met with the lawyer, we found out that Grandpa wanted my sisters and me to live together for a month to repair our relationships. Then, and only then, could we own Lost Canyon Ranch. Floyd will make the final decision."

Knox pinched the bridge of his nose. "You've been hiding that fact all this time? What if the lawyer decides you haven't earned it? Then I was here for nothing."

Pain flickered in her eyes. "I wasn't the only one keeping secrets. I saw your notes next to your designs. You're buying the land for Scarlett Sutherland. How could you? You know how I feel about that family. Evelyn is the only reason I'm selling to you. She left me with little choice."

"I couldn't tell you. I signed a nondisclosure agreement. As the developer, I wasn't at liberty to tell anyone, especially not the current landowner."

"That's how you see us?" Her arms moved wildly as she spoke. "As a developer and a landowner?"

"No, that's not what I meant."

"It's the first thing that came to your mind." Lainey rose quickly, her chair skidding across the wooden floor. Keeping her back to him, she walked to the sink and looked out the window.

"Come on, don't be this way." He stood and moved behind her. He reached out to touch her shoulders, then decided against it. "I care about you. I …"

Her braid moved from side to side as she shook her head. "There's a reason you can't finish the sentence. You don't know what you want. I thought it might be me."

She quickly moved away from him and marched to the mudroom. She yanked her winter coat off the hook and grabbed a hat, scarf, and gloves that were lying on a bench.

She shoved the clothes on in fast, frantic movements. "I'm going to the barn to check on Cocoa."

"Of course. Instead of finishing a conversation with me, you want to run off to be with your horses." His voice rose. "Have you ever realized you treat your horses better than the people around you?"

Anger flared in her bright blue eyes before she slammed the door behind her.

Knox gripped the counter for support, his knees almost buckling beneath him. He might get everything he'd wanted, and yet, it felt like he'd already lost everything.

CHAPTER
Sixteen

THE UNFORGIVING wind whistled in the darkness. Lainey wrapped her scarf more securely around her neck and marched into the barn. Tears slipped down her cheeks. This time, she didn't try to stop them. She let them flow, giving in to the full extent of her emotions.

A sob escaped her throat. Knox had never seen her as anything more than a landowner. All the conversations, the flirtatious banter, their kiss … it had all been part of his plan. A means to get what he wanted.

She'd been so stupid. So reckless with her heart to fall for someone who would eventually leave. She should have known better. If her own father hadn't wanted to stick around for her, why would Knox? A man who didn't owe her anything?

Growling, she turned on the overhead lights and kicked a tin can, sending it clattering across the floor. It rolled down the aisle, landing near Rebel's open stall door.

No, no, no. She hurried over to the stall.

Empty.

Her heart beat wildly in her chest. Neither Cheyenne nor Quinn could've taken Rebel anywhere. They'd gone inside the house after court, just like she had. Maybe one of the ranch hands had an explanation. She dialed Amos's phone. "Did you see anyone in the barn with Rebel before you left?"

"Sure did. Knox was grooming him."

Her lips parted. Knox? Had he put Rebel back in the stall and forgotten to lock it? Or had he done it on purpose? He could have been the one causing havoc all this time.

It didn't seem likely, but it was possible. She wiped at a fresh set of tears streaming down her cheeks.

"Lainey? You still there?" Amos's voice came over the line.

"Yeah."

"What's wrong?"

"Rebel isn't in his stall."

Amos blew a deep breath into the receiver. "We'll send out a search party first thing in the morning."

She shook her head, even though Amos couldn't see her. "No, I have to go now."

Rebel could get stuck in the snow and freeze. The meteorologist said the area might get up to twenty inches tonight.

She couldn't let anything bad happen to Grandpa's horse. She was about to lose the ranch. She couldn't lose Rebel too.

She ended the call without giving Amos an explanation. The old man was right; she should wait. Or at least get someone to come with her. But Amos and Travis were safely in their trailers already. Cheyenne wouldn't be much help in the woods. And if Lainey went inside the house to get Quinn, then she'd have to confront Knox again. If he was the saboteur, he'd only stall her.

There were no good options at this point. Every minute she wasn't looking for Rebel would delay her search. She had to go alone.

In a hurried rush, she packed overnight supplies and prepared Jingle Bells for the trip. A UTV would be faster and warmer, but if she had to go into the woods, a horse would navigate the trails better. As long as she had a flashlight.

Minutes later, she rode along the ranch's perimeter. Snow dove down from the black sky, swirled through the frigid air, and stuck to the frozen ground.

The pastures would be buried within the next few hours.

"Rebel!" She swept the flashlight from left to right.

There were no signs of him anywhere. No prints in the newly fallen snow. No noises of distress. Filled with dread, she directed Bells toward the woods. The mare halted.

"Rebel is out here somewhere. Please find him."

Bells stepped forward onto the trail.

"Good girl."

For the next mile, the night was eerily quiet. Many animals had no doubt taken shelter from the storm. Lainey kept the flashlight on the path. Even with a light, the mare slowed to a trot, her large thighs noticeably moving up and down beneath Lainey's legs.

High-pitched howls broke through the silence.

A wolf pack.

Could their den be close by? She peered through the darkness, looking for similarities to the place where she'd found the cub. In the darkness, it all looked the same.

Lainey gripped the reins tighter. What had she been thinking, coming out alone?

She'd hadn't been thinking; that was the problem. She'd let her emotions get the best of her, and she'd made a very bad choice.

The only people who knew she'd left the house were Knox and Amos. Would Knox realize she hadn't come inside yet? Would he tell Cheyenne and Quinn that she was missing? If he was the saboteur, then probably not.

But he couldn't be, could he?

Ugh. She should've told someone besides Amos that she was going out to search for Rebel. She should've *called* Quinn. That way, she wouldn't have had to go inside to face Knox. Why hadn't she thought about that before?

She pulled on the reins, signaling Bells to stop. She could try to call her sister now. At least to let her know where she was. With trembling hands, she took off her gloves, stored the flashlight in her left coat pocket, and pulled out her cell phone.

No service.

Grimacing, she held the phone higher. "Come on. Just one bar," she pleaded.

Nothing.

The howls grew closer. Up ahead, the bushes rustled.

Jingle Bells sniffed at the air and backed up a few steps.

The blood ran out of Lainey's face. A wild animal was in the bushes. Was it the wolves or another animal? She tried to stuff her cell phone in her pocket and grab the flashlight again. But the phone slipped through her cold fingers, falling with a light thump in the snow. She couldn't get off the horse to pick it up, not when a predator lurked behind the bushes.

She swallowed against a dry throat and put a hand on her rifle. As a last resort, she would use it if she had to. She grabbed the flashlight, shining it in the direction of the noise.

A large gray wolf slowly crept around the bush. Its wild eyes gleamed in the darkness.

Lainey's heart hammered against her chest. It had a white stripe down the middle of its face. Could it be the same mother wolf she'd encountered with Knox?

Somehow, that day felt like a lifetime ago.

Letting out a high-pitched neigh, Bells tried to back up, but Lainey tugged on the reins, keeping her horse in place. She had to think through her options. If they made a run for it, the wolf would most likely catch them. Horses were faster than wolves but keeping a fast pace on uneven terrain at night would be hard for Bells. And the wolf had an advantage—this was its natural habitat. Getting caught would result in one or both of them dying.

And yet, if they stayed still, the wolf might attack them. If that happened, she'd have to use her gun. Guilt pricked her conscience. Those poor cubs would be without a mother. But it was Lainey's life or the wolf's. Maybe the mother wouldn't attack?

Or there was option three—she'd wait a little longer. Just in case, she tucked the flashlight beneath her armpit, keeping it zeroed in on the wolf as she pulled her rifle out.

The wolf growled, exposing its sharp teeth.

Lainey rubbed her horse's shoulder in a slow circular motion. The mare's body was trembling.

Seconds later, Jingle Bells lifted her front legs and kicked at the air.

Lainey clutched the pommel and held on.

Bells lowered to the ground and lifted her legs again.

This time, the angle was too steep. Lainey slipped off and dropped to the ground as Jingle Bells dashed off, disappearing into the woods.

Sprawled on the ground, pain sliced through Lainey's hip. Adrenaline shot through her veins, amping her survival instincts into full force.

The wolf stepped closer. It stood two feet away; its teeth still bared.

Her heart beat so fast it felt like it would explode. She couldn't wait any longer. If the wolf decided to attack, she only had seconds left.

She reached for her gun, which had fallen with her, and prepared to shoot. Her whole body shook. She had to stay calm.

Just then, the wolf began to retreat.

Behind Lainey, something small and fast whizzed

through the air. Seconds later, a dart struck the wolf in the shoulder. The wolf opened its mouth, trying to bite at the dart before it moaned and slumped to the ground. Someone had stunned it with a tranquilizer.

Lainey dropped the rifle, then collapsed to the ground. Her eyes fluttered close for a second. *I'm alive.*

A man wearing a black face mask and puffy winter coat stepped out from behind a large pine tree.

Who was he? Had he found Jingle Bells and come to look for her rider?

He stood rooted in place and crossed his arms. "Hello, Lainey. It's been a while since we've seen each other."

That voice. It sounded familiar, but where had she heard it?

Before she could contemplate his identity for too long, he quickly broke the distance between them. He grabbed her wrists and forced her to stand.

"Let go of me." She tried to wrestle out of his grip, but he was too strong.

"Of course, you're doing this the hard way. You leave me no choice." He jammed a dart in her neck and let go.

Pain shot through her neck. Her head felt woozy, and her limbs went limp. She crumpled to the ground as her world suddenly went black.

———

Groaning, Lainey opened her heavily lidded eyes. Blurry stars danced across her vision. She blinked repeatedly until her vision cleared. Where was she?

Her cheek rested against a bear fur rug. She must be lying on the floor. But why?

And what was wrong with her mouth? She moved her tongue, trying to touch the roof of her mouth but tasting cloth instead.

There was a bandana tied around her head, preventing her from screaming. Instinctively, she tried to remove it, but her hands wouldn't budge. She had to adjust her body to see that her wrists were bound together with a thick rope. Her ankles were tied together too.

Panic seized every inch of her body. Her head throbbed as she tried to remember what had happened.

She'd had an argument with Knox. Then, she discovered Rebel missing. She went to look for Grandpa's horse when she ran into … the wolf.

It took a moment before she could remember the rest.

The man wearing a ski mask had shown up, tranquilized the wolf, grabbed her and … drugged her.

Dread tingled her nerve endings. She'd been kidnapped.

Whoever kidnapped her had to be the saboteur.

Her heart picked up speed. She had to escape. She scanned the space, looking for a way out. Thin rays of moonlight shone through a window across the room.

Wait a minute. She'd seen this room before.

The pounding in her head made it difficult to think. When had she been here? The memory came back like a slow freight train chugging up a steep hill.

The bed. The bear fur rug.

She was in the bedroom of the shack.

Now that she knew where she was, she could run in the right direction after she made it outside. *If* she made it outside.

Voices rose from the living room.

She struggled to one elbow and pushed off the floor, moving to a sitting position. She strained to listen.

"How long before Lainey wakes up?" a woman asked.

Lainey sucked in a breath, almost gagging on the bandana. She would know that sultry voice anywhere.

Scarlett.

Shock radiated through Lainey's limbs. She should have known Scarlett was in on the sabotage as soon as she'd found out Scarlett was Knox's client. Still, it was hard to believe. Sure, they weren't close friends like they'd once been, but wreaking havoc on Lost Canyon Ranch and kidnapping Lainey meant that Scarlett harbored a lot of anger toward her.

"It won't be much longer," the man from the woods replied. "Once she wakes, let me drag it out for a while. I'll enjoy watching her squirm."

"I owe you that much. You've been quite helpful to me, causing much more trouble for Lost Canyon Ranch than I could've done alone," Scarlett said. "But keep in mind, we have a purpose to fulfill."

"Of course." The man chuckled—a low menacing laugh that caused chills to ripple down Lainey's spine.

It suddenly clicked. That laugh belonged to Damian Hart.

A lump lodged in her throat. So, there *were* two people working together. Knox had been right, after all.

Oh, Knox. Her chest ached with longing. She'd really screwed things up. Instead of getting upset and leaving the house, she should've told him why she felt so hurt. Because deep down, she cared about him. A lot.

"You really think this will work?" Damian asked.

"Yes. I'm positive."

How in the world had Scarlett and Damian met and started working together? A postal servant from

Cherry Creek and a music agent from Nashville wouldn't easily cross paths.

Think, Lainey.

It must have been *People.* Scarlett had been reading the article about Cheyenne and Damian's breakup the day Lainey had stopped by the post office. Had Scarlett connected with Damian after that? But why? There were too many loopholes to fill in.

Scarlett's voice took on a triumphant tone. "When Cheyenne and Quinn find the body, they'll be so devastated that they won't want anything to do with Lost Canyon Ranch. They'll sell it in a heartbeat."

The body.

Her body. Nausea rolled through her stomach in violent waves, threatening to make her throw up. They wanted to kill her.

"I can't believe I had to tranq the wolf first," Damian said.

"You should've let the beast kill her. Then there wouldn't have been any blood on our hands." Scarlett's displeasure was evident.

"I told you already. The wolf was backing away. It wasn't going to harm her. The only reason I tranquilized it was so it wouldn't attack me when I grabbed Lainey," Damian explained.

"Oh, sure. She might be good with horses, but

wolves too? That's absurd." Scarlett snorted. "You wanted to bring her here so she could see you."

"I don't care if you believe me or not. But am I pleased with the circumstances? Yes. She needs to know how she ruined my life."

"Whatever. Say what you need to say. Go check on her."

Lainey leaned to one side, sliding to the floor. She squeezed her eyes shut and focused on keeping her breathing steady.

Heavy footfalls stomped toward the bedroom. The door opened.

Seconds later, Damian spoke. "She's still out."

He closed the door behind him.

Relief flooded through her, if only for a moment. She didn't have long before he'd come back, expecting her to be awake. She had to escape.

———

A sudden rustling sound came from outside the window, followed by a low grunt.

Lainey pushed herself to a sitting position and stared in the direction of the noise.

A black shadow appeared behind the frosted windowpanes. With the full moon shining above, the figure was bathed in an ethereal glow.

Her body stiffened. Was it a ghost? *The* ghost?

Although she'd truly been frightened of the ghost story and the unexplained light as a girl, she'd never actually believed there was a supernatural being in the shack. Now the possibility felt very real.

Or maybe the drugs hadn't worn off yet. Maybe the shadow was a figment of her imagination.

A large hand pressed against the glass, quietly pushing the window open. A cold gust of wintery air drifted inside as a man peeked inside the room.

Her eyes widened. Unless ghosts had superpowers, he was definitely a real person. Where had he come from? How had he known she'd been kidnapped? Was he planning to save her?

Before she could contemplate it any further, the stranger maneuvered his large body through the opening and lowered himself to the floor with surprising agility.

He took a few steps forward, his face coming into view. Deep linear scars ran from his forehead to his cheek. The rest of his face was covered by a long, unruly beard. "I'm not going to hurt you. I'm here to help."

She nodded. Her heart thudded hard and fast against her chest. Scarlett or Damian could check in on her at any second, and then they'd both be in danger.

The man moved swiftly across the room and knelt down in front of her. He untied her wrists and unraveled the rope around her ankles. Then, he unknotted the bandana and gently pulled it out of her mouth.

She rubbed the raw skin around her wrists. "Thank you."

"We need to hurry. I'll lift you up and push you out the window."

Behind them, the door swung open. Scarlett and Damian stepped inside the room, each holding a gun that they pointed at Lainey. Their attention wavered for a second, a flicker of surprise crossing their faces as they assessed the newcomer and the open window.

"Both of you, kneel on the floor," Scarlett commanded. "Now."

Lainey reached for her pistol. Her hip holster was empty.

A wicked smile spread across Scarlett's face. "Do you really think we'd let you keep a weapon?"

The blood drained from her face. She had no choice but to fight Damian and Scarlett. Her fingers twitched with nervous anticipation, but she wouldn't act just yet. "I'm surprised to see you in Cherry Creek, Damian. According to you, this town, and my family's ranch, is way beneath your standards. If I remember correctly, you called your family's ranch the crème de la crème of ranches in Tennessee."

"I'm here for your sister. Cheyenne doesn't

belong in this Podunk town. She belongs with me in Nashville."

"Is that so? Then why doesn't she want to be engaged to you?"

His jaw tightened.

She'd hit a nerve. But at least she had him talking.

He stepped closer, keeping the gun pointed at her chest. "You convinced Cheyenne to break it off with me. Didn't you?"

So that was why Damian believed she'd ruined his life. He thought she was behind the breakup. It made sense, given their last conversation, but little did he realize that Cheyenne made her own decisions. "My sister didn't want to marry you. I had nothing to do with it."

"Don't lie to me." Damian spoke through clenched teeth. "Cheyenne agreed to marry me. Then she came back to your sorry excuse of a ranch, and *you* put ideas in her head." He sneered. "When you're dead, she'll come to her senses. She'll see that she made a mistake."

She tensed her leg muscles. With Damian this close, it was time to act. She balled her fingers into fists and lifted the knuckle of her pointer finger slightly higher than the rest of her fingers. She jammed a powerful uppercut into his rib cage, twisting her wrist so the lifted knuckle hit a pressure point, while she pushed the gun off to the side.

Groaning, Damian bent forward.

The bearded man sprang into action. Staying low, he lunged at Scarlett with his burly arms outstretched. His hands caught hold of her ankles and yanked her to the ground. The force of the fall must have caught Scarlett by surprise. She pressed the trigger on her gun, sending a bullet into the air. Pieces of wood sprinkled down from the ceiling.

The distraction of the gunshot gave Damian enough time to compose himself. He stood to his full height and aimed his gun at Lainey's head.

While sucking in a breath, she jumped up, lifted her right leg, and swung a powerful roundhouse kick at his hand.

Damian let go of the gun. It slid across the floor.

Before he could chase after the weapon, she extended her arm and punched him in the nose.

He stumbled backward, cupping his face as blood gushed onto his lips and chin.

"You'll pay for that." Letting go of his nose, he threw a punch at her stomach.

She tried to block the jab but wasn't fast enough. His blow knocked the wind out of her. She doubled over, gasping for breath.

He punched her in the same spot, the force propelling her to the floor. Something sharp tore into her leg. She winced and glanced down. A fire poker lay beside the bed. Whoever had been sleeping in the shack had probably kept it beside the bed in case they ever needed to protect themselves.

Loud scuffling came from the other side of the room. But she couldn't focus on what was happening with them. She had to take care of Damian first. She grabbed the fire poker and rose to her feet.

Scarlett screamed, sounding like a vicious animal attacking its prey.

Damian turned his head to look at Scarlett.

He quickly realized his mistake. Too late, he shifted to face Lainey.

She struck the side of his head with enough force to knock him out.

His body teetered, then collapsed.

Her gaze swung to the other side of the room. She repositioned the fire poker in her sweaty palms, ready to strike again.

The bearded man lay crumpled on the floor with Scarlett towering above him, a gun pointed at his chest.

"No! Don't kill him. It's me you want. Let him go. Please." Lainey's voice trembled.

"If you put down the fire stick and tie him up so we can finish our business, I won't kill him."

With shaky hands, Lainey lowered the steel rod to the floor and picked up the rope.

"Tie it around his wrists and ankles," Scarlett instructed.

"OK."

Scarlett cocked the gun and pressed it against the back of Lainey's skull. "Don't try anything funny. I'll know if the knots aren't tight. And I won't hesitate to shoot him."

Lainey's heart raced. She had no choice but to tie up the only person who could help her. But she wouldn't give up. Somehow, she would find a way to get free.

CHAPTER
Seventeen

BENEATH HIS THICK coat and hat, Knox shivered uncontrollably. It wasn't just the zero-degree temperatures causing his body to shiver, it was the thought of Lainey out in the woods, alone.

An hour ago, Jingle Bells had shown up at the ranch. The horse had paced across the front yard, neighing until he'd heard her and come outside. He'd immediately alerted Cheyenne and Quinn. As soon as the horse had their attention, Bells turned in the direction of the woods as if she'd wanted them to follow her.

They tacked up two of their other horses and took off. Knox rode Jingle Bells.

So far, there were no signs pointing to Lainey's whereabouts. The snow didn't help matters. It covered any footprints that might have been on the ground. At least Bells seemed to know where she was going.

Behind him, Quinn sniffled. "I'm so worried. I can't believe she went off to find Rebel tonight. I mean, I can, this *is* Lainey we're talking about, but in a storm like this? And without telling us?"

"We'll find her," Cheyenne said, the tremors in her voice giving away her fears.

Knox took a deep breath. In and out. In and out. How had Lainey and Jingle Bells become separated? Was she hurt?

He gripped Bells's reins tightly as regret weighed heavily on his shoulders. He'd had the opportunity to stop Lainey, and he hadn't. He'd let her storm off to the barn. Because he was mad too. She should've told him she didn't own the ranch.

But now, none of it mattered.

If he had the chance to tell her of his true feelings, he would. Scratch that. *When* they found her, he would tell her. He had to think positively. To imagine anything else was too much to bear.

Quinn let out a gasp. "That's the shack up ahead, and there's light coming from it. Do you think Lainey could be inside, waiting out the storm?"

A flicker of hope ignited in his chest. And yet, doubt and fear crept in just as quickly. "Maybe the person who'd been living in it is back."

Jingle Bells sniffed the ground. She sniffed the air, then she turned off the trail, toward the shack.

Knox exchanged looks of concern with Cheyenne and Quinn. It was dangerous to go off the path at night. But Bells had brought them this far. They had to trust the horse's instincts. Lainey must be inside.

"What if she's hurt?" Quinn asked. "What if that's why Jingle Bells came back and Lainey didn't? What if she's—"

"We're almost there," Cheyenne interrupted. "We'll find out soon enough."

His heart picked up speed. What would they find when they got inside?

———

Lainey's hands trembled as she finished the knots around the bearded man's wrists and started tying rope around his ankles. She worked slowly, trying to buy time. Talking had kept Damian occupied, maybe it would work on Scarlett too, if only for a few minutes so Lainey could make a getaway plan.

"Why can't you build a resort on your parents' property? That sounds like something they'd love to do."

Scarlett let out a low hissing sound. "Of course, Knox couldn't keep a secret from you. I should have fired him as soon as he started falling for you."

Lainey ignored Scarlett's comment. "Why not somewhere else? Someone else's ranch besides mine?"

Scarlett hesitated. "Oh, I have many reasons. And taking your land feels … justified."

Lainey's fingers stilled. "Justified?"

"We were best friends. Then you started dating my twin brother, of all people, and it was like I didn't exist anymore. Like I wasn't good enough for you. In the end, my brother wasn't good enough for you either." The barrel of the gun pressed harder into Lainey's skull as Scarlett continued. "After you came back from college, people started talking about you like you're some kind of magical horse whisperer, like your grandpa. I'm over it."

They had? Lainey's mind reeled. She couldn't focus on that, though. Scarlett's reasoning made one thing quite clear—she had been the mastermind behind the sabotage. She'd obviously cut the fence before she saw the magazine article on Cheyenne and Damian. But then, somehow, Scarlett had connected with Damian and convinced him to help her. It couldn't have taken much convincing, considering his own anger toward Lainey. "How do you and Damian know each other?"

"I met him two years ago when he visited Cherry Creek with your sister. My parents invited them over for a dinner party. I'm surprised you didn't hear about it." Scarlett paused. "You know what? You wouldn't have. Because you'd just kicked Damian out of your house. They came to the party and then went home on a private jet."

Lainey didn't have to see Scarlett's face to know she was sneering. Scarlett took any opportunity to gloat when she knew something others didn't.

Scarlett tapped the gun hard against Lainey's head. "Go faster. You're stalling."

Swallowing hard, Lainey finished tying the rope around the stranger's ankles.

Using her free hand, Scarlett curled her finger, motioning for Lainey to follow her. "Get up."

"Where are we going?"

"Just do what I say. You don't need answers to everything."

Lainey exchanged a look with the bearded man.

His eyes were filled with concern. "Fight," he said under his breath, quiet enough that Scarlett couldn't hear.

Nodding, she left the room. Her legs wobbled as she walked into the main living quarters where she and Knox had spent the night together.

"Sit down," Scarlett ordered.

Instead of listening, Lainey remained standing. This was it. Scarlett would shoot her from behind before she had a chance to make things right.

With her sisters. With Knox. She should've

listened to him. He was right. She did treat horses better than people.

She'd had everything right in front of her—her sisters, the horses, and a man she'd started to care for deeply. It was those relationships that she should've been grateful for, that she should've held on to, not the ranch. Not the land. How had her priorities gotten so mixed up?

Behind her, Scarlett cocked the gun.

Lainey prepared to turn around and fight.

Voices rose from outside, then all went quiet.

The door swung open.

Knox rushed inside with Cheyenne and Quinn, their faces crimson from the cold.

For one brief moment, everyone remained motionless. Her gaze flickered to Knox.

"No one move." Scarlett's command sliced through the room.

"What's going on?" Knox asked, his eyes locked on the gun.

"You messed up, that's what's going on. You had one job to do. Convince them to sell. And you couldn't do it. I had to take matters into my own hands."

His Adam's apple bobbed up and down. "The land is yours," he said. "Lainey agreed to sign the papers."

"Oh, sure. Likely story."

"It's true," Lainey confirmed as she slowly turned around.

Scarlett eyed them warily, distrust evident in her scrutiny. "It's too late now. This isn't going to end well for any of you. Looks like a triple murder-suicide will work."

"Don't you dare." Damian entered the room, pressing a palm to the spot on his head where Lainey had struck him. In his other hand, he carried a gun. "That wasn't in our plans. Cheyenne's coming with me."

Cheyenne took a hesitant step backward.

Scarlett laughed. "*Our* plans? We didn't have plans, Damian. They were always mine."

His eyebrows furrowed together.

A smug smile spread across Scarlett's face. "Over-confidence is obviously your downfall. It's why you thought you could cheat on Cheyenne and get away with it. I knew you'd be the perfect accomplice, so self-absorbed that you wouldn't pick up on what was really going on."

Lainey balled her hands into fists, preparing to attack. Better to make the first move when Scarlett was preoccupied.

"What is really going on, then?" Knox asked.

The proximity of his voice startled Lainey. He'd slowly inched closer and was now standing a few feet away.

Scarlett lifted her chin. "I could care less about owning a dude ranch resort. It's just a cover so I can launder money from my *other* business."

Lainey thought hard, working to put the details together. *Other* business? A business where Scarlett needed to launder money to keep from getting caught.

Flashes of a news headline resurfaced: "Fist Fights at the Outlaw Saloon at an All-Time High. Cherry Creek's Sheriff Blames Drug Use."

Lainey gasped. "You're the one distributing drugs. You're the reason Jingle Bells had cocaine in her system. But how?"

"That's right. Took you long enough to figure it out. I injected cocaine into an apple and told Tori to give it to the horse."

Anger tore through Lainey's body. Using it as fuel, she swung a left hook at Scarlett's cheek, then followed with a right backfist at the hand that held the gun.

It didn't work. Scarlett clutched the gun as tight as a vise. Her green eyes filled with rage. She directed the pistol at Lainey and pulled the trigger.

Lainey tried to move, but her body froze.

Knox jumped in front of her, pushing her out of the way as Quinn ran at Scarlett.

Their movements distracted Scarlett enough that the bullet whizzed past Lainey's ear, broke through the window, and shattered the glass. Sharp pieces flew across the room.

Lainey winced as a large piece of glass cut into her cheek. She pulled it out. Blood dripped down her face.

Knox seemed torn between going after Scarlett and rescuing Cheyenne, whom Damian had grabbed from behind and was dragging toward the open doorway with his hand clasped over her mouth.

Another shot rang out, followed by a blood-curdling scream.

Lainey's ears rang as she turned around to see what had happened.

Quinn was on the floor, clutching her leg. Blood poured out of a wound on her thigh.

"No!" Lainey screamed.

Rage replaced anger, sending her into a fury. She broke the distance between her and Scarlett, barreling into her and knocking them both to the ground. She wrestled the pistol out of Scarlett's hand.

Knox sped across the room and grabbed it. He stood with his legs shoulder-width apart and pointed the gun at Damian, the only other person who had possession of a weapon. "Don't move a step farther."

While Damian was distracted for a second, Cheyenne elbowed him in the ribs, grabbed the gun, and escaped from his hold.

Knox turned toward Scarlett. "Don't you dare hurt Lainey, or I'll shoot you."

Lainey's chest rose and fell. Relief washed through her. She smiled at Knox. *My, oh my, how far the city boy had come.*

CHAPTER
Eighteen

ON CHRISTMAS DAY, Lainey looped her arm around Quinn's waist and led her to the front porch. As Quinn eased down onto the swing, Lainey draped a thick blanket over their laps. They sat in silence, the hum of voices inside the house rising and falling. Word had spread quickly about the kidnapping and shooting. Throughout the week, townspeople had visited in waves, bringing meals and desserts.

They'd also wanted to see Josephine. Mom had flown back to Montana as a surprise, only to be more surprised by the recent events.

This morning, more townspeople had come over to finish decorating the house for Christmas. Almost everyone had shown up at one point—except the Sutherlands. According to Georgia, the family was lying low, still in shock over Scarlett's criminal behavior.

Scarlett and Damian were currently being held at the Carbon County jail, waiting for their trials.

It was hard to fathom that they'd actually planned on murdering Lainey and that they could've killed her sisters and Knox too.

But they'd all made it out alive. They'd retold the story numerous times. Everyone wanted to hear it firsthand. Most people weren't surprised that Lainey had put up a good fight and defended herself. They'd seen her in karate, beating most of the class in sparring.

What did shock them, though, was that Knox had stopped Damian from kidnapping Cheyenne and that he'd threatened to shoot Scarlett.

When Georgia heard this, she'd jumped up and down and clapped her hands. A goofy grin spread across her face before she'd said, "I know what Knox's nickname is. Has anyone ever heard of sugar plum phyllo kringle?"

No one spoke.

She'd pushed her glasses higher up on her nose. "It's a pastry. After being baked, the bread looks delectable. It has this lovely golden-brown color, and it's sprinkled with confectioner's sugar." She paused for a moment before she continued. "The inside is filled with cream cheese, dried cherries, dried apricots, raisins, and walnuts."

Everyone had looked at her, waiting for an explanation.

"The inside of the sweet pastry is made up of harder and crunchier ingredients. Just like Knox. He has a grit and tenacity that no one could see, until now." Georgia beamed. "Long story short, I'll call you Sugar Plum."

Knox had seemed pleased to finally have a nickname. Or maybe it was because his actions had given them the upper hand to stop the criminals and call the sheriff.

By the time the sheriff had arrived, the bearded man was gone. It would always bother her, not knowing who he was or where he'd come from. A hunter passing through? A nomad traveling across the country?

Quinn pulled the blanket up to her chest. "It finally feels like Christmas."

Lainey frowned. "If only we had Rebel home safe." The likelihood of finding him alive after the snowstorm was slim, but she wouldn't give up hope.

We need a miracle, Grandpa would've said. *Life is full of miracles. You just have to keep your eyes open.*

"Are you OK?" Quinn asked.

"I wish Grandpa was here."

"Me too."

"He would've loved having all these people at the ranch on Christmas Day."

Quinn nodded. She shifted slightly, wincing as she readjusted her wounded leg.

"Do you need more medicine?" Lainey asked.

"No, not yet. It doesn't hurt too much." Quinn expelled a heavy breath. "All that money Grandpa gave me for a coach, and I can't even perform at the Denver Stock Show. That could've been my ticket to the Olympics."

"I understand you're disappointed, but it could've been worse." Lainey wrapped her arm around Quinn's shoulders. Her sister had lost out on a major opportunity, but she could've lost her life. All because Scarlett wanted a dude ranch resort to hide money from her illegal activities.

Lainey should've seen the signs. But they'd known each other their whole lives. Her old friend had changed subtly over the years, making it difficult to detect Scarlett's malicious motivations hidden beneath the surface.

At least Scarlett, hoping for some leniency from the court, had turned in the donation box with the money still in it. The total had amounted to three thousand dollars.

Unfortunately, it wasn't enough to start the horse training business. But Lainey had put it into savings for when the time was right. One day, she'd start the business just like she'd hoped.

Cheyenne opened the screen door and stepped out onto the porch, followed by Floyd. "We come bearing gifts of hot chocolate." She squeezed onto the swing beside Lainey and handed each of them a mug topped with whipped cream and sprinkles.

"My favorite." Lainey took a sip of the warm frothy drink, eyeing the lawyer over the rim of her cup.

Floyd leaned his lanky frame against the wooden porch railing. "Would you look at that? The three of you snuggled together on a porch swing." He smiled, the creases around his eyes becoming more pronounced behind his glasses. "Your grandpa would be proud. You've had to work through quite a few obstacles in the last month." He counted off on his bony fingers. "Getting sued, sabotage, and a developer trying to convince you to sell."

Lainey's cheeks warmed at the last *obstacle*. Knox had been quite the opposite. A blessing in disguise.

Floyd pushed off the porch railing. "You have undoubtedly earned the ranch. It's yours for the keeping."

A wide smile spread across Lainey's face. "Oh, thank you, Floyd." She rose and gave the lawyer a long hug. "That's the best present you could give us."

"I agree," Quinn said from the swing.

Cheyenne stood, shaking Floyd's hand.

His cheeks turned pink. "Merry Christmas." He rocked back on the heels of his boots. "I better get home to the missus. She's probably wondering what's taking so long."

Lainey waved goodbye and settled onto the swing beside Quinn.

Cheyenne continued standing. She clasped her hands together. "I have something I want to tell you both." A nervous smile spread across her face. "I'm not going back to Nashville. I'm staying in Cherry Creek."

Quinn's lips parted. "Are you serious?" She paused for a moment as Cheyenne nodded. "I'm so happy to hear that."

"Are you sure that's what you want?" Lainey asked timidly. Their relationship was still on the mend, so Lainey had to proceed with caution, but she had to question her sister. Cheyenne should pursue whatever was in her heart. "You love singing. You shouldn't give it up because your first agent was a sabotaging kidnapper."

"I agree. I won't let Damian ruin my career. Now that he's locked up, I feel much safer. I wish I would've told you I'd seen him at the Blade Parade and during the horse clinic, but I thought I was seeing things. The sabotage had me on edge. And I never would've believed that he'd show up in a town he despised."

She took a breath. "Anyway, I've been thinking about the money Grandpa gave me. I'd like to open my own studio in Cherry Creek to record and teach voice lessons. We'll use the initial revenue to help you start your business, Lainey."

Moisture built in Lainey's eyes. "You'd do that?"

"Yes, definitely." Cheyenne beamed.

Quinn shook her head. "Actually, you don't have to do that."

"Why not?" Lainey and Cheyenne asked simultaneously.

"Remember those pictures and videos of Cocoa and Nutmeg that I took?" Quinn smiled. "I posted them on social media and asked for help in taking care of them. They've gone viral. So far, they've made ten thousand dollars."

Lainey shifted in the swing to look at Quinn fully. "Are you serious?"

"Yes, people loved them. You could post new videos to market your business now that you have a following."

Lainey laughed. *A following?* She'd never cared about things like that, but if it would help her business, she had to go for it. "Thank you so much, Quinn. I can't say no to extra revenue."

"Is that so?" Cheyenne looked over her shoulder

as Knox's truck pulled into the driveway. "I wanted to run an idea by you, but I'll let Knox do it."

Lainey's heart wobbled at his name. Now that Scarlett was no longer his client, there wasn't any reason for him to stick around. His job was in Seattle.

Knox stepped out of his truck, wearing boots over his jeans, a brown suede coat, and a matching scarf. He'd shaved the stubble on his jaw, and his hair was perfectly styled.

Her stomach did airy flip-flops. Wow, he cleaned up good.

As he approached, he held out an open hand. "Let's go for a walk. I know how hard it is for you to sit still for too long."

Grinning, she descended the stairs, curiosity bubbling in her chest.

Knox reached for her hand, entwining their fingers. He led her away from the house, stopping inside the barn. He loosened the scarf around his neck. "I have a new client who would like to own the dude ranch resort."

Lainey's eyebrows pinched together as she waited for him to explain.

"Cheyenne thinks it would make a great addition to Lost Canyon Ranch."

"Addition? As in, not tearing down what's already here?"

"Exactly." Knox smiled. "The resort could be

located by the shack. Then the shack could be the check-in and check-out office. The guest cabins would be built around it. It would all be in the woods, which would offer more privacy for the guests and for you."

"Wow, you've already thought this through, haven't you?"

"What can I say? I'm a planner." He smirked. "The other positive to the resort is that it would bring in a lot of revenue. Cheyenne wants to add a stage where local singers or famous stars could perform. That would be a great way to market it once it's open."

"I don't know … The guests would still be staying on our property …"

"*Paying* guests. And with it being farther away, they wouldn't interfere with your ranch or the animals. Although, I would suggest using some of your horses for trail rides."

She twisted her lips. "Does this mean that Mt. Point Development would own part of our land, after all?"

"No. I will. I'm opening my own development company right here in Cherry Creek. You and your sisters would be my first clients." Knox set his hands on her waist. "It'll be a lot of work, which is exactly what I didn't want when I found someone special to share my life with. However, I've realized that not all my plans have to happen the way I imagined. I'm still getting exactly what I wanted in the end."

"And what's that?"

A slow grin spread across his handsome face. "Falling in love with you."

His words knocked the wind out of her. A lump formed in her throat. Moisture built in her eyes. "I … I love you too."

He wrapped his arms around her lower back, pulling her close. "Does this mean you'll let me build the resort?"

She let out a playful sigh. "You won't take no for an answer, will you?"

"I've told you that from the beginning."

Lainey laughed. "All right, all right. You can build it." She brought her lips to his, letting the kiss simmer slowly as reality settled in.

Knox and Cheyenne were both staying. They were building a dude ranch resort. Her and Grandpa's dream of starting the horse training business would finally come to fruition.

And best of all—she would gain a man who made her heart swell, a man who pushed her out of her comfort zone, and a man who encouraged her to see that change could be good.

———

On New Year's Day, Knox leaned down from the saddle and patted Nutmeg's shoulder. Cocoa rubbed his head against his mother's leg, standing tall and healthy. The trek up the mountain had been good exercise for them.

Knox peered at Lainey out of the corner of his eye. She looked so beautiful sitting on Jingle Bells as she gazed out at the snow-covered hills—her posture straight, chin lifted, a braid sneaking out of her cowgirl hat, and loose strands cupping her rose-colored cheeks. His chest constricted. She was his. His strong-willed, confident, cowgirl.

"This view never gets old," Lainey said.

"It really doesn't." He didn't take his eyes off her.

With the horses standing side by side, she nudged him with her elbow. "Don't be so cliché."

"Don't pretend you don't like my cliché compliments."

She rolled her eyes.

He leaned over and kissed her cheek. So much had changed since he'd first come to Cherry Creek. Leaving Mt. Point Development. Moving to Montana. Loving a woman like Lainey, and becoming a better man.

Navigating this new year would be interesting. He already had plans for the future—plans for his business and plans with Lainey. But if there was one thing he'd learned this year, it was to stay open-minded to other paths. In the end, it wasn't about the outcome; it was the journey that mattered. Experiencing this life with Lainey would be nothing short of an adventure.

Movement at the edge of the woods caught his attention. His brow furrowed. He tipped his cowboy hat lower, shielding his eyes from the bright rays of sunshine. "Did you see that?"

She nodded, her gaze unwavering from the spot.

Bushes and trees leaned off to the side as a black leg stepped forward.

Knox held his breath. It wasn't … It couldn't be …

The black-and-white horse broke through the woods. Rebel caught sight of Lainey, his ears perking as he galloped toward them.

Knox grinned. *Unbelievable.*

Squealing, Lainey hopped off Bells and held her arms open wide. "Come here, boy."

Rebel halted in front of her, lowered his neck, and nuzzled his nose against her face.

Tears glistened on her cheeks. "Oh, Rebel, I thought something bad had happened to you. I can't believe you're OK."

Knox shook his head in wonder before sliding off Nutmeg. "Hey there, buddy."

At the sound of Knox's voice, Rebel glanced at him. The horse moved over and pressed his muzzle against Knox's chest. When Rebel lifted his neck, slobber caked Knox's coat.

He laughed. "This brings back memories."

Smiling, Lainey stepped back, her eyes roaming over the horse. "I'll have to call the vet for an internal examination, but there are no obvious wounds." She noticeably swallowed. "It's a miracle. He found his way home."

Knox slipped his arms around her waist. He pulled her close and lifted her off the ground. A slow grin spread across his face. "So have I, Lainey."

Dear Reader

Dear reader,

Boy, did I challenge my limits with this novel. Before I wrote *Hometown Roots*, I had no experience with horses or ranches, and I'd never been to Montana. I needed to lay a strong foundation for the upcoming books in the series, which will feature Cheyenne and Quinn. I had to weave in details about the mystery of the missing person, the haunted shack, and a cast of minor characters who will play larger roles in the upcoming novels.

Finding a way for Lainey and Knox to fall in love also had its own challenges. They are both stubborn people who had their lives mapped out. But their plans didn't work out the way they'd hoped. That was the real love story, wasn't it? Finally putting their own ideas aside to see that they could choose a better path, together.

Like Lainey, I don't like change. I grew up in Iowa, got married in Iowa, imagined raising my kids and retiring in … you guessed it, Iowa. So, when my husband got a job in Florida, all my plans were uprooted. But living in a new state, in a very different climate, my family has grown stronger in ways I never thought possible. Moving gave me the spark of an idea to write about a couple who could grow stronger individually and collectively when faced with life-altering changes.

I hope Knox and Lainey's love story touched your heart, and I hope you enjoyed your time at Lost Canyon Ranch. There is *so* much more to come. This is just the beginning of our stay in Cherry Creek.

Warmest regards,
Crystal Joy

P.S. If you enjoyed *Hometown Roots*, I would appreciate it if you would help others enjoy this book too.

Lend it—I have many readers who tell me how much they like sharing books with their friends or relatives. So, please do. Read it, share it, and talk about it. Nothing makes my heart happier than readers connecting.

Recommend it—Please help other readers find this novel by recommending it to friends, to readers' groups, and on social media.

Review it—Please tell other readers why you liked this novel by reviewing it on one of the following websites: Amazon or Goodreads.

If you are part of a book club, there is also a reader's guide for *Hometown Roots*. Feel free to email me with questions before you get together!

Email: crystaljoybooks@gmail.com.

Thanks for reading!

Also By Crystal Joy

Enjoy small town romance? The Homeward Bound series is for you!

A sweet series with a dash of suspense. Wounded characters struggle to let go of the past, forgive themselves, and find love in Maple Valley, Iowa, a quaint town located by the Mississippi River.

Shackled Heart, Book 1 (MacKenna and Charlie)
Shattered Heart, Book 2 (Amanda and Ethan)
Stained Heart, Book 3 (Grace and Caleb)

Enjoy reading about real-life relationships? These love story collections are for you!

Each book has seven short stories featuring real

couples. Some couples end up together, some don't.
You won't know which until you finish their story.
Who will end up broken-hearted? Who will find their
happily-ever-after?

*Completely Captivated: Fictionalized Love Stories
aboReal-Life Couples*

*Completely Yours: Fictionalized Love Stories about Real-
Life Couples*

Acknowledgments

What would I have done without all of you? Honestly, I would've stopped writing this book. There is no way I could've published this novel without your help. I am forever grateful for each and every one of you!

Mike, Landon, Zoey, and Savannah—thank you for joining me at the local rodeos, going horseback riding, and for enduring my new obsession with horses!

Mom and Dad—thank you for your endless support with my writing career and connecting me with readers from all over. Mom, your encouragement and belief in this book always kept up my spirits when I needed it most.

Janice—you are the BEST editor and critique partner there is! I loved your idea for Georgia to give everyone in Cherry Creek nicknames. I had a blast creating the nicknames, especially the long list of possible names for Knox. You're such a gem!

Research team—Jean, JoAnne, Jennifer, Megan and Pam, Paige, Bek and Siri from Believe Ranch and

Rescue, Heidi and Randy, Terry, Julie, Trudi, Kenzie, Kristin, Sean, and Brett—YOU ARE AMAZING! I had a million questions, and you took the time to answers my phone calls, emails, and texts. You are the reason this book is realistic. You are the reason Lainey came to life on the page. You are the reason the plot made any bit of sense.

Beta readers—Mike, Mom, Lauren, Cathie, Claudia, Stacie, Paige, Jenna, Jordon, JoAnne, Marilyn—Wow. Just wow. Thank you for taking the time to read my rough draft(s) and giving me such inciteful feedback!

Crystal's Crew—I used so many of your brainstorming ideas in this book. You are my favorite Facebook group ever!

God—thank you for bringing all these special people into my life. I'm forever grateful for the opportunity to pursue my dream of being an author.

Readers—thank you for reading my books and sharing them with others! I can't wait to hear what you thought of *Hometown Roots*!

Reader's Guide

1. Who is your favorite character from *Hometown Roots*? Which character do you relate with the most?

2. Lainey is very traditional. What Christmas or holiday traditions do you enjoy with your family?

3. Knox and Lainey have different lifestyles. What attracts them to one another?

4. Georgia struggles to pick a nickname for Knox. What nickname would you chose for him? What are your favorite food nicknames?

5. If you went horseback riding at Lost Canyon Ranch, which horse would you want to ride: Rebel, Nutmeg, or Jingle Bells? Why?

6. Both Lainey and Knox have plans for their lives that don't turn out the way they'd imagined. What plans haven't worked out in your life? Did they work out better or worse?

7. Lainey and Cheyenne's relationship is difficult. What brings them together by the end?

8. If money wasn't an issue and you could hire a build-to-suit developer, what kind of business would you want to build or renovate?

9. Did you predict the correct saboteur(s)? Who else did you consider as a possibility?

10. Cheyenne and Quinn are the lovely heroines in books two and three of this series. Which sister are you most looking forward to seeing as a main character? Why?

About the Author

Crystal Joy writes stories about two unlikely people falling in love. She is a grassroots kind of author who can often be found at local events with her books. Meeting readers is her favorite part of being a writer and fuels her extrovertedness in a way that sitting at a computer—all by her lonesome—cannot.

When she's not writing, she's spending time with her husband and three children at the pool, the beach, or anywhere outside in Florida.

If she can't meet you face-to-face, Crystal would love to connect with you in other ways, so visit her website at www.crystaljoybooks.com, visit her Facebook page at https://www.facebook.com/CrystalJoy Books, or email her at crystaljoybooks@gmail.com.

Made in the USA
Columbia, SC
28 July 2024